*** !TRUMP! ***

In Three Acts

by

Robert M. Lebovitz

ISBN 978-0-9971209-2-9

PREFACE

Of all the domestic elected individuals who have(had) made themselves ripe for political satire, Donald J. Trump certainly is one of the most fertile. His voluminous official pronouncements via tweets and his frequent public impostures have yielded a bumper crop of stand-ups and send-ups. While obviously fictional in its details of public/private speech, the thematic arc of *** !TRUMP! *** is based upon real political events and notable public figures. Reports in the media have provided the quotes that are seeded within the text.

An apology is due, however. This isn't a finished piece. How could it be? The Trump story is still developing. Many newsworthy events are yet to come, along with much debate as to whether he's helped or harmed, whether his presidency is one to be celebrated or overcome. As of this writing, it is December 2019 and President Donald J. Trump has been impeached. The 2020 electoral circus has barely begun. Whether or not he is acquitted, whether or not he wins reelection, whether or not he even runs are unimportant at this juncture. Be he historically rejoiced or reviled, be he lauded or defamed in future analyses, he has changed American politics. Indeed, he may have changed America. As Shakespeare wrote: "The evil that men do lives after them; the good is oft interred with their bones." Be that as it may, he may soon have his Decimus. He most certainly will have his Marc Antony, as dramatized here via Lindsey Graham's supportive paean in Act Two.

This satirical *** !TRUMP! *** is in the form of a three-act play. It's envisioned as a take-off on the speeches given and music played at political events to animate supporters. Whereas several opera/operetta musical themes are explicitly called for (or implied), the bulk of the dialogue is rhythmic verse, forgoing melody. A full musical treatment is yet to be written, in other words. However, see "Musical Performance Notes," below.

The play's actual closing curtain is in the future, as are our individual and collective ends. The election of November 2020, not his impeachment in 2019, would seem to be the fitting climactic. Yet, even that would be only partially anticipatory. Much more is sure to unfold thereafter, whatever the determination of the electorate. Think of this early version as the Christmas gift that was intended for 2019 but may be rewrapped for presentation on another, and, perhaps, yet another Christmas.

RML

Also by Robert M. Lebovitz:

To Be: Birth of Rational Termination
A novel of co-opted virtual unreality, a dramatization of deepfake technology being used not to augment but to replace sentient beings ... to replace our selves.

We Never Do Wednesday's: Apart Together - A Couple's Alzheimer's Journey
A novel of acceptance.

NUTS! A Fable
A fantasy of the rationalized destruction of tradition, based upon evident social/political trends.

America Lost
Stories of Troublesome Times.

The Mocking of the President
Satire, spoofs, & parodies featuring: "Trumpfinger - The Great Deceiver" & "WHO's In Charge?"

MUSICAL PERFORMANCE NOTES

This is the script of an augmented lyrical stage piece. Only a few explicit musical references are provided, such as, for example, the operatic themes utilized. Below, however, is a listing of the songs to be performed and, in lieu of a full score, suggestions (in italics, e.g., "// *Money, Money, Money*") as to the intended style and rhythm. This provides a useful guide to the shape of the drama.

ACT ONE

MONEY, SON, IT'S MONEY: Fred Trump, Young Donald // *Money, Money, Money*

MILLIONAIRE'S SON: Young Donald // *Fortunate Son*

MONEY, YES, IT'S MONEY: Mature Donald (Reprise of above)

BOLLYWOOD MUSIC AND DANCE: Instrumental // *Fire Night*

LOVELY WOMEN: Trump // *Oh, Pretty Woman*

UP TIMES, DOWN TIMES: Workmen, et al. // *Good Times and Bad Times*

MONEY, MONEY, MONEY, MON-EY: Instrumental // *TV "Apprentice" theme*

I'M GOING TO BE THE CHOSEN ONE: Apprentice Candidates // *Number One*

CHANGE IS IN THE AIR: Trump // *Revival*

OUR COUNTRY'S MOOD NEEDS CHANGING: Trump // *The Times, They Are A-changin'*

ALL YOU NEED IS FEAR: Miller // *Love Is All You Need*

DON'T BE SMUG TONIGHT: Clinton // *Bad Moon Rising*

TRUMP JUST WANTS TO HAVE FUN: Moderators // *Girls Just Want To Have Fun*

ACT TWO

TRUMP JUST WANTS TO HAVE FUN (Reprise): Offstage ensemble

DON'T BE SMUG TONIGHT (Reprise): Offstage ensemble

SOMBER WEDNESDAY: Clinton // *Gloomy Sunday*

BOLD TRUMP: Trump Supporters // *Wild Thing*

BUILD THAT WALL: Trump Supporters // *The Wall*

ARRIVAL OF THE QUEEN OF SHEBA: Instrumental, from the opera *Solomon* by Handel

I'VE HAD FUN AND GAVE THEM PAIN: Trump // *Fire and Rain*

MY WAY: Instrumental // *My Way*

STORMY WEATHER: Trump Supporter // *Stormy Weather*

DIRTY DEAL: Cohen // *Dirty Deeds*

SMEAR'S THE NATURE OF THEIR GAME: Melania // *Sympathy for the Devil*

PRESCIENT, POTENT PRESIDENT Graham and Fox Friends. Based upon "Model of a Modern Major General" from *Pirates of Penzance* by Gilbert and Sullivan

IT'LL BE SIMPLE: Kushner // *It's So Easy*

RUSSIAN DANCE: Instrumental, from *Nutcracker* by Tchaikovsky

STAND WITH ME, RUDY: Trump, with Giuliani // *Stand By Me*

I SAW IT IN THE FAKE TIMES: Trump // *Heard It On the Grapevine*

WE'LL MEET AGAIN: Pelosi, with Reporters // *We'll Meet Again*

ACT THREE

I'LL HANDLE HIM (THEM): Trump // *Surrender*

KOREAN MINYO (FOLK SONG): Ethnic Ensemble, "Saetaryeong" Song of the Birds

MY BUDDY JUST SENT ME THIS LETTER: Trump // *The Letter*

WHAT DID THEY FIND?: Jordan // *Sixteen Tons*

IT'S NOISE: Pompeo // *Cum On Feel the Noize*

PLAGUEY, PROLIX PRESIDENT: Schiff. Based upon "Model of a Modern Major General" from *Pirates of Penzance* by Gilbert and Sullivan

GOOD TIME FOR A WHITE RALLY: Miller // *White Wedding*

THE BEST DEFENSE IS ALWAYS TO ATTACK: Trump. Based upon "Der Vogelfänger bin ich ja," from the opera *Magic Flue* by Mozart

DIE WALKÜRE, ACT THREE OPENING: Instrumental, from the *Ring Cycle* by Wagner

GÖTTERDÄMERUNG, FINALE: Instrumental, from the *Ring Cycle* by Wagner

EPILOGUE

IT'S UP TO YOU, REAL AMERICA: Bearded Man // *Mrs. Robinson*

!TRUMP!

A satirical musical
in three acts

Book and lyrics by
Robert M. Lebovitz

December, 2019

SETTING:

> TRUMP FAMILY RESIDENCE, QUEENS, NEW
> YORK; VARIOUS CONVENTION SITES,
> BRIEFLY. PRIMARY ACTION IN WASHINGTON,
> D.C.

TIME:

> LATE 1960'S TO PRESENT

PROLOGUE

ON RISE

BEARDED MAN IN DARK BLUE SUIT, LIT FROM KNEES
UP.

BEARDED MAN
Thank you for coming. What will be presented
here is political satire. It's based upon
real events, of course — what people of whom
you know have said and done — but fictional.
There are good reasons for us to inform but,
fiction being fiction, to entertain will be
enough.

> (He slips a red rubber ball over his
> nose).

Every era must have its comedians to make us
laugh at what may not be truly funny.

> (He pops the red ball off then on
> again while making a silly face and
> showing off his overly large shoes,
> which an expanded spot has now
> revealed.)

See? You do laugh. A little, at least. My
friends, what we offer we hope will be
entertaining but less silly. The trick, as
you must know, is to discern who are comedic
by intention and who come to wear its
costume despite and perhaps as the very
opposite of their wish. Keep that in mind,
even after you leave.

Thank you. The performance will now begin.

ACT ONE

STAGE DARK. OVERTURE THEN LIGHTS UP ON A HOME
OFFICE WITH IMPRESSIVE DESK, SEVERAL CHAIRS
IN FRONT, ETC. **FRED TRUMP** STANDS ALONGSIDE,
MILDLY AGITATED AND GESTURING, A TELEPHONE
HANDSET TO HIS EAR. **MATURE DONALD TRUMP** IS ON
A RAILED BALCONY UPSTAGE. BOTH ARE DRESSED IN
DARK BUSINESS SUITS, EXCEPT THAT DONALD'S
COAT IS OPEN AND HIS IS A VERY LONG, RED TIE.

>(FRED TRUMP pulls handset away
>momentarily and looks out, lips
>tight. He puts handset back firmly
>against his ear.)

FRED
Yes. But look, I've had to deal with his
kind for as long as I've been in this town.
More than I wanted, really. New York's not
Kallstadt. I ... Okay. But tell him ...
Fine. I understand. But you tell that Little
Mister Silverstein what's on the table and
that he can take it or walk away.... Sure I
mean it.... Well, make him think I do, then.

>(MATURE DONALD, folds arms across his
>chest and lifts his chin as he looks
>down.)

FEMALE VOICE OFFSTAGE
Fred? Donald's here. He wants to see you.

FRED
(To VOICE) Just a moment. (Into phone) Tell
him, and make him believe it. He'll cave.
They always do.... (Laughs) Yes. Half a
bagel is better than none.

ACT ONE

(**COLLEGE-AGE DONALD** walks in, jacket
and shirt collar open, tie askew. He
lays several textbooks on the desk
and pushes them away.)

FRED

(Putting down phone) Hello, Donald. (Looks
at him, then at watch.) This is a surprise.
Everything okay at school?

YOUNG DONALD

Yes, Sir. I thought I'd spend this weekend
at home.... We were talking, about what
we're going to do after graduation. Most of
the guys are going into their families'
businesses.

FRED

That's wise. I'm looking forward to someone
in the family taking over.

YOUNG DONALD

I'd rather make it on my own, Dad. Do big
things so people say "That's *Donald J.
Trump!*"

(FRED motions for him to sit.)

FRED

Plan big things, sure, great and grand
things, but only if they'll turn a profit.
My advice is very, very simple, son: Make
money. That's all that's worth fighting
about. The rest is derivative. Understand
what I'm saying?

YOUNG DONALD

(Nods a yes) But how? (Gestures toward
texts). Is it in there?

ACT ONE

FRED

Partly, but just the mechanics. Making money
is an art not a science, Donald. Do it
anyway you can. Money is what makes
civilization work. Without it, all we'd have
is what we could gather up, hunt down, or
trade for.

(YOUNG DONALD nods without speaking.)

FRED

Good. Money and indoor plumbing changed more
lives than have all the books and deep
thoughts. More than most grand things, too.
(Laughs) Think of money the way a farmer
thinks of seed: It's basic, everything comes
from it, and you need it to get more. But
use other people's. You see? Stand to win
without ever having to risk a loss.

YOUNG DONALD

Will they let you?

FRED

Let you? Certainly they'll *let* you. They'll
let you because they want to make money
themselves! You can always count on self-
interest, Donald. When you make money for
yourself, it's easy to convince people you
can make money for them. Remember, it's not
how much you have but how much they *think*
you have. The appearance of success makes
people want to get in on your game, play on
your team. You can use that.

YOUNG DONALD

I don't think I could do that yet.

ACT ONE

FRED

Probably not. You have to practice, work at
it for a bit. But you'll find it's like
being on stage in the theater. It's not who
you are but who you can make people think
you are. Power works the same way and comes
with the money. They — money and power —
feed each other. And when you have both ...
Well, that's beautiful. Be clever. Don't do
like Freddy. Aim high. Even run for Mayor
when you've got enough. Win or lose, that
would be good for business.

FRED
"MONEY, SON, IT'S MONEY"

All in all, it's simple, Donald:
Set your goal and play the role.

Most work all day, some work all night
To stay alive and light their lights.
That's not the way.
Then even so, they have to fight
To get each week what is their right,
Their measly pay.
For you, son, the better plan
Is make yourself a wealthy man.
You'll never really work at all,
Just milk the game and have a ball.

Money, son, it's money,
Makes life sunny.
This is a rich man's town.
Money, my boy, think money,
Sweet as honey.
New York's a rich man's town.

ACT ONE

Plan ahead and chart your own way.
Just make a lot of money
And don't care what they say.

A man like me is hard to find.
Not many have a Trump's clear mind.
So do as I say.
I'll set you up to make start.
Don't waste your time on being smart.
Does not pay.
I'll give you cash to be on your own.
You'll soon need more, so get a loan.
To build your brand light up your name
And make the suckers play your game.

Money, son, it's money,
Makes life sunny.
This is a rich man's town.

Money, boy, think money,
Sweet as honey.
New York's a rich man's town.
Just look ahead and chart your own way.
Work on making lots of money
And don't care what they say.

YOUNG DONALD
Actually, I can already see what it's going
to be like for most of those guys in my
class. They talk a lot about the easy way,
the family jobs. They won't deserve what
they get, but they'll get it anyway and
think they're so smart.

ACT ONE

YOUNG DONALD

It's not fun to jump out of bed
Then sit by some snot who'll get pushed
ahead.
That's so bad.
I'll float my own deals, raise lots
more cash,
Then crank it up and make a splash.
Maybe make them mad.

With little in of my own
I'll promote big plans, get bigger
loans.
I'll use their money from the start
And use my own to play the part.

Money, yes, it's money,
Makes life sunny.
It's a rich man's town.

Money, yes, it's money,
Sweet as honey.
New York's a rich man's town.
I'll look ahead and chart my own way.
I'll make a lot of money
And not care what they say.

YOUNG DONALD (AND FRED) DUET

Money, Dad(yes), it's money.
Makes life sunny.
This is a rich man's town.

ACT ONE

Money, yes! It's(Think) money,
Sweet as honey.
New York is a rich man's town.

I'll(Just) look(plan) ahead and chart
my(your) own way.
Right, I'll(just) make a lot of money,
And not(don't) care what they say.

> (FRED pulls out a bundle of bills
> from a drawer, throws it onto desk.)

FRED
Put that start to good use, Donald. And
remember: It's sometimes easier to make
money when times are bad then when times are
good. Fear and greed are what drive most
people. Look for them. You can use that in
others to make profits for yourself.

SCENE SHIFTS TO A COLLEGE DORM ROOM WITH
SEVERAL **CLASSMATES** IN SPORT COATS LOUNGING
ABOUT (UPSTAGE LEFT), SMOKING, AND TALKING.

> (YOUNG DONALD moves downstage, closes
> then moves upstage to join them,
> slowing as he approaches. CLASSMATES
> pay him scant attention as they laugh
> and interact.)

IMAGES OF TALL BUILDINGS APPEAR ON UPSTAGE
WALL, BLENDING OVER ONE ANOTHER, EACH
PROGRESSIVELY MORE GRAND.

> (YOUNG DONALD faces toward these,
> then straightens his shoulders and
> turns toward his peers upstage.)

ACT ONE

YOUNG DONALD
"MILLIONAIRE'S SON"

I'm not like them, part of a long line
Who are happy to run back to home.
I'll not do that. I'll make my own dime,
Do whatever, to make it on my own.

But in a way that's me, that is me.
I am a millionaire's son.
*In a way that's me, that **is** me.*
I was born a fortunate one.

They'll never fight strangers to become super rich.
They'll get paid for working for their dads.
They'll spend sweaty nights with some society bitch,
Marry well, and want just what they've had.

Well, that won't be me. In no way is that for me.
I want more than being a millionaire's son.
That won't be me. In no way is that for me.
I'll be a notable one.

    (CLASSMATES clap each other on the back and drift offstage left,

ACT ONE

(ignoring YOUNG DONALD, who turns
toward audience.)

YOUNG DONALD

I'll put my name all over this town.
Trump! Bright and large, in brass and
in stone.
I won't care that they once put me down
When I watch them scramble to live in
what I own.

That'll be me. That'll be me.
I'll be more than a millionaire's son.
That'll be me. Yes, that'll be me.
I'll be the notable one.

Some people moan when tax time comes
around.
Not me. I'll have other bills to pay.
Uncle Sam could get his in the end
But that'd be some far, far off day.

That's what's for me. That'll be me.
I'll be more than a millionaire's son.
That's what's for me. That'll be me.
I'll be the notable one.

That's what's for me. That'll be me.
I'll be the notable one.

YOUNG TRUMP IS ISOLATED BY NARROW SPOTLIGHT,
WHICH DIMS. SPOT COMES UP ON THE MATURE TRUMP,
STANDING OPPOSITE.

ACT ONE

IMAGES OF HOTELS AND OFFICE BUILDINGS COVER
THE UPSTAGE WALL. TRUMP TOWER (NYC) COMES TO
DOMINATE.

TRUMP
"MONEY, YES, IT'S MONEY"

A man like me is hard for them to take,
Because they think I'm just a fake.
But that's not bad.
Dad always said to go for gold.
There's nothing wrong with being bold.
Anything less is sad.

I've done well and made quite a name,
Next comes politics, a true Trump game.
Soon I won't need to work at all,
Just fly around and have a ball.

Money, yes, it's money,
Makes life sunny.
This is a rich man's town.
Money, yes, it's money.
Can flow like honey.
New York is a rich man's town.

I've looked ahead,
Did business my way!
I make a lot of money and can be Mayor
one ripe day.

I look ahead
And always chart my own way.

ACT ONE

*It's certain, I'll make a lot more
money,
And become Governor one day.*

SPOTS OFF.

THE TRUMP TAJ MAHAL (ATLANTIC CITY) APPEARS ON
UPSTAGE WALL, MANY VIEWS OF WHICH ARE SHOWN
THROUGHOUT THE DANCE SEQUENCE:

DANCE COMPANY
(**BOLLYWOOD ENSEMBLE** number -
colorfully costumed dancers with
lively sitar and tabla music.)

ENSEMBLE EXITS TO MUSIC. STAGE DARK.

UPSTAGE WALL SHOWS AN IMAGE OF A GRANDIOSE
AUDITORIUM SET UP FOR MISS UNIVERSE PAGEANT.
A CURVING RAMP EXTENDS FROM HIGH UPSTAGE LEFT
TO STAGE CENTER FRONT.

(One voluptuous girl after another
struts down the ramp. Most, but not
all, are in Miss Universe Pageant
bathing suits. The mature DONALD
TRUMP, in formal attire, watches from
downstage right. He stops some then
casts them aside to continue his
perusal.)

TRUMP
"LOVELY WOMEN"
*Shapely women, I love to watch them
walk.
Shapely women, the kind that hate to
talk.*

ACT ONE

(To one) Lovely woman,
We've searched the world for those like
you.
You can believe that what I say is
true.
I never lie!
Stately women, I love them tall.
Stately women, one is sure to accept my
call.

(To another) Lovely woman,
You're the best of all today.
Please come to me and stay.
I'll make it pay!

(To another) Sexy woman, you're my
style.
Sexy woman, I'll make it worth your
while.
Sexy woman, don't say no to me.

(To another) Sexy woman, don't you see?
Sexy woman, if you play this part,
Sexy woman, it could be your start.
Because I need you, I'll treat you
right.
You're so lovely. Please spend the
night.

      (He shrugs off refusals and continues
      along the group.)

ACT ONE

Ambitious women, I know what's in their
hearts.
Ambitious women, they're looking for
their starts.

(To another) Lovely woman,
You're the best on stage today.
Won't you come to me and stay?
Well, at least, for one sweet day.

Lovely woman, you're my style.
Lovely woman, it'll be worth your
while.
Lovely woman, don't say no to me.
Lovely woman, don't you see?
Lovely woman, if you play this part,
Lovely woman, it could be your start.

What's that in your eyes I see?
The sign that you agree?
Yes, you'll spend some time with me
And be my lovely woman!

> (TRUMP takes her arm and they start
> offstage.)

Shapely women, I love to watch them
walk.
Shapely women, the kind that hate to
talk.
Stately, sexy, ambitious, lovely women!

ACT ONE

STAGE GOES DARK WITH THEIR EXIT.

TRUMP ENTERS, IN BUSINESS ATTIRE. IMAGE OF
TRUMP'S TAJ MAHAL REAPPEARS, IN FULL GLORY,
THEN GRADUALLY CRUMBLING. SOUND OF VOICES
ARGUING. **WORKMEN**, **CONTRACTORS**, **BUSINESS MEN**
IN SUITS, ETC. IN A BUSTLING MASS ABOUT
TRUMP. OFFSTAGE SOUNDS OF HEAVY
CONSTRUCTION.

WORKMEN, CONTRACTORS, BUSINESSMEN
"UP TIMES, DOWN TIMES"

In his days back in school
His father told what it took to be on
top.
He's been there more than once,
And more than once he's had to deal
with a flop.
No matter what his critics say,
There's no way he is ever going to
stop.

> (Throughout, *ad lib* pieces of
> business as TRUMP moves about the
> stage interacting with WORKMEN
> carrying clipboards and rolled-up
> plans. Several CONTRACTORS approach
> him and, handing him bills, are
> rebuffed. WORKMEN - bricklayers,
> carpenters, electricians - carrying
> materials and/or finished work pass
> across stage. Some — mostly minority
> — drop their loads and offer out
> their hands to no avail. More
> BUSINESSMEN enter from stage left,
> handing TRUMP legal papers.)

ACT ONE

WORKMEN, CONTRACTORS, BUSINESSMEN

Up times, down times,
Trump has had his share.
But knowing other peoples' money gets
burned
Doesn't mean he has to care.

While still young, he bought and built
Not worried if the projects didn't gel.
Tax law being a bible to him,
He'd flash by Go and never think of
jail.
The trick, he knew from Fred,
Was to get quite big, become too big to
fail.

Up times, down times,
He's seen sun and he's seen rain.
But whenever a deal went real bad,
It was the investors who felt the pain!

When casinos and hotels failed
He never would bat an eye.
Living large was to be his way,
To escape looking like he was living a
lie.
So what if bankers came and took
control?
He found many more flush fish to fry!

ACT ONE

Good times, bad times,
Always managed to get his share.
And seeing peoples' money get burned
Didn't give him reason to care.

Up times, down times,
He managed to get his share.
And knowing other peoples' money got
burned
Didn't mean he had to care.

FRED TRUMP APPEARS ON UPSTAGE BALCONY ONCE
MORE. HE POINTS TO DONALD.

FRED TRUMP
You've made your money. To hell with them,
sonny. Now you need more. Look around and
you'll see. Money is power, that's the key.

Focus on that and you'll even the score. Be
Mayor, or even Governor! Why not? I sweated
to get mine. Having it all is your lot.

TRUMP
(Who hasn't really heard, but is thinking.)
Mayor? Governor! Yes, why not me? Or even
more! President! I've enough for that,
you'll see.

> (**MAN IN GARISH SUSPENDERS** approaches
> TRUMP.)

TRUMP
(To MAN IN SUSPENDERS) I've formed a
committee, Larry, to run for President. I
know just the party that'll suit me and the
policies that'll sweep me in.

ACT ONE

Perot will love me. Oprah will support me.
Politics and business operate the same: Both
run on money going to the money, for the
money. See?

I'll even marry! But, win or lose, it'll pay
to advertise! I'm adept at that game.

STAGE OPENS. RAUCOUS PARADE OF **DELEGATES** WITH
REFORM PARTY "TRUMP!" PLACARDS, SOME WITH THE
APPEARANCE OF NEWSPAPER FRONT PAGES. OTHER
PLACARDS HAVE PICTURES OF JESSE VENTURA IN
WRESTLING TIGHTS.

TRUMP
(To DELEGATES) Few are big enough to oppose
me! I'll give free health care for everyone.
I'll reduce, then end the national debt.
Mine will be a beautiful, beautiful world.
I'll make it all work. I understand good
times and I understand bad times. No
politician is going to do as good a job as
Donald J. Trump!

MILLING CROWD WITH PLACARDS THINS. THOSE WITH
TRUMP'S IMAGE ARE MUSCLED OFF THE STAGE.
STUDIO CAMERAS COME IN FROM EITHER SIDE.

(TRUMP shrugs, smiles broadly, then
waves studio cameras closer.)

TRUMP
No matter. My hotels and casinos benefited
big time, big time. The Reform Party has no
future. I was just something to see. Media's
the thing. I've got time and I've got many,
many more deals to make. Someday, maybe,
I'll try again. I could do that, and win!

(TRUMP sits at an ornate table and
straightens his tie.)

-19-

ACT ONE

OFFSTAGE: REPEATED SNATCHES OF TRUMP'S
"APPRENTICE" SHOW THEME, WITH FADE.

Money, money, money, mon_ney, Oh. Yeah.

TV CAMERAS ON HEAVY STANDS MOVE IN FROM LEFT
AND RIGHT. **APPRENTICE CANDIDATES** - MEN AND
WOMEN IN BUSINESS ATTIRE - CROWD IN FROM
EITHER WING, FORMING TWO VAGUELY SEPARATE
CLUSTERS IN FRONT OF TRUMP. THEY SHIFT ABOUT,
JOCKEYING FOR POSITION.

TRUMP
Over here! Point those cameras here, at me,
not at them.

APPRENTICE CANDIDATES
I want to be your apprentice. I can! I will!
Please. Please!! Here's my plan. Here's my
goal. Let me be the one.

APPRENTICE CANDIDATES
"I'M GOING TO BE THE CHOSEN ONE"
The stress is fierce,
But I'm pushing on.
I'm going to be the chosen one.
I'm not the kind of guy (girl)
Who gives up when talk gets tough.

Hearing that my team has won
Is worth suffering the bad.
The smaller that our group becomes
The more reason to be glad.
I'll be the kind of girl (guy)
Who shows how good is never enough.

ACT ONE

(Several, in the clusters in front of
TRUMP, hang their heads, turn, and
leave the stage.)

The critiques are cruel,
But I'm pushing on.
I have to be the chosen one.
I'm not the kind of guy (girl)
Who gives up when talk gets tough.

I can deal with pressure
It's what will make me strong.
I'll be just as vicious
And make clear who did it wrong.
I'll be the kind of girl (guy)
Who gives it back when talk gets rough.

(A few more leave, as above.)

The stress is fierce,
But I'm pushing on.
I intend to be the chosen one.
I'm not the kind of guy (girl)
Who'll give up when talk gets tough.

Every time that another is gone,
She (He) walks away with her (his) sad
head down.
No way I'll let that be my last step.
I'll focus on what will be my best
step.
Cut the nut, get on top somehow.
That's the way to play my cards now.

ACT ONE

*Might be a show, but it is no damn
game!
The host is a bully, so I'll do the
damn same!*

*The critiques are cruel,
But I'm pushing on.
Can't be one who hears "You're fired!"*

*The stress is fierce,
But I'm pushing on.
Must be the one who's praised and
hired.*

(As above.)

*Despite the stress, I see what it does
take,
Be unconcerned when others do break.
The taking down of foes and friends is
A basic part of Apprentices business.
Do it fast before it becomes their
turn.
Talking tough is what I have learned.
Winning isn't just a good and fine
thing,
Winning's the rule, the essential, the
prime thing!*

(A handful of CANDIDATES are left.)

ACT ONE

The critiques are cruel,
But I'm pushing on.
Can't be one who hears "You're fired!"

The stress is fierce,
But I'm pushing on.
Must be the one who's praised and
hired.

(Fade) The stress is fierce,
But I'm pushing on.
I'm going to be the chosen one.
I'll not be the kind of guy (girl)
Who gives up when talk gets tough.
No, I won't be the guy(girl)
Who gave up when talk got tough.

TRUMP
(To no one in particular) You're fired!!!

(TRUMP rises from behind table)

TABLE IS REPLACED BY A VERY ORNATE ONE
SURROUNDED BY FLAGS.

(TRUMP goes to desk, surrounded by
STAFFERS AND STENOS, and faces a
clutch of **PHOTOGRAPHERS**. TRUMP waves
and smiles, then approaches one of
the many flags and salutes it, as a
premeditated photo-op. He moves to
center stage, followed by
PHOTOGRAPHERS.)

ACT ONE

TRUMP

Now's my time. I've got the exposure. I've got the backing. I've got the money. Conservatives love me. I can fund my own campaign. To hell with the politicos! I'll make having no experience be my strength. I have so, so much to say. I'll drain the swamp and make Washington work again!

(TRUMP paces among the crowd.)

TRUMP (WITH CHORUS)
"CHANGE IS IN THE AIR"

Tell me, can't you sense it?
Change is in the air.
Can you, can't you hear it?
Change is in the air.

People are tired of rules from DC,
Tired of dictates from smug elites.
I'll give them an alternative.
They'll turn out and flood the streets.

Tell me, can't you sense it?
Change is in the air.
Can you, can't you see it?
Change is in the air.

They're fed up with the Left's lies.
It's time to lead this fight.
I'll make the run for President
And energize the Right.

ACT ONE

Tell me, can't you sense it?
Change is in the air.
Can you, can't you feel it?
Change is in the air.

People tired of rules from Washington,
Tired of dictates from smug elites.
I'll give them an alternative.
They'll turn out and flood the streets.

Tell me, can't you sense it?
Change is in the air.
Can you, can't you smell it?
Change is in the air.

I need you to support me,
I need you to wave the flag.
I'll make it fly proud again,
Instead of treating it like a rag.

(Chorus, with fade.)
(Can you, can't you hear it?
Change is in the air.
Can you, can't you see it?
Change is in the air.
Can you, can't you feel it?
Change is in the air.
Can you, can't you smell it?
Change is in the air.
Can you, can't you sense it?
Change is in the air.)

ACT ONE

LIGHTS ON DESK DIM, ISOLATING TRUMP LOOKING
BACK AT WHERE IT WAS. STAGE GOES DARK.

LIGHTS UP ON A DIVIDED STAGE. STAGE LEFT -
REPUBLICAN CONVENTION FLOOR WITH TRUMP ON
DIAS AT REAR, SMILING OUT AND WAVING.
CONFETTI, STREAMERS, AND DETRITUS ALL AROUND.
TRUMP SUPPORTERS IN PREPONDERANCE OF RED
HATS, SWEATERS, SHIRTS, ETC.

STAGE RIGHT - LARGE MEETING ROOM, WITH A
CLUSTER OF **CLINTON SUPPORTERS** SHOWING A
PROMINENT DISTRIBUTION OF BLUE. THEY STARE AT
AND OVER VIDEO SCREENS — CARRYING A FEED OF
THE REPUBLICAN CONVENTION — WHICH ARE LOW
DOWNSTAGE BUT FACING UPSTAGE.

> **TRUMP**
> This is a moment of crisis for our nation.

> (TRUMP SUPPORTERS go quiet)

> **TRUMP**
> America is far less safe and far less
> stable. This is the legacy of Hillary
> Clinton: Death, destruction and terrorism
> and weakness.

> **TRUMP SUPPORTERS**
> Booooo! Lock her up!

> **TRUMP**
> There can be no prosperity without law and
> order.

> **TRUMP SUPPORTER**
> Bring it, Donald

> **TRUMP**
> One more child to sacrifice on the altar of
> open borders. (In a steady recitation:)

ACT ONE

Dallas. Georgia, Missouri, Wisconsin,
Kansas, Michigan, and Tennessee.
Louisiana!!! I'll restore law and order. We
need a wall!

TRUMP SUPPORTERS
Build that wall!

TRUMP
Nobody knows the system better than me[sic].
That's why I alone can fix it.

TRUMP SUPPORTERS
Build that wall! Build that wall!

TRUMP
Our steelworkers, our miners are going back
to work again.

TRUMP SUPPORTERS
Bring back our jobs! OUR jobs!

TRUMP
America first. We will make America great
again!

TRUMP SUPPORTERS
Keep them out. Send them back. America for
Americans!

TRUMP
We don't win anymore, but we're going to
start winning again. I'm with you, the
American people.

ACT ONE

TRUMP
"OUR COUNTRY'S MOOD NEEDS CHANGING"

I'm glad that you've come
To cheer me on here,
To support the big changes
That I plan for next year.
If I don't get it done now
You'll have much more to fear.
We must turn them out, our country's
worth saving.
They claim she can't lose
But that's not really so clear.
Our country's mood needs changing.

The pundits and writers
Who predict my big loss,
Can't grasp that they've fallen
Deep in the swamp's stagnant moss.
All proud of the lies
That they so love to toss,
They can't see it's those they back who
are losing.
The ones who are out
Will soon be the boss,
If our country's mood will only start
changing.

They've pulled us far left
And we've seen liberties lost.
There's a line in the sand,
We mustn't let it be crossed.

ACT ONE

If we let them win now
There'll be a grim cost.
I will lead and show we're not fading.
Our country needs help,
Needs to regain what was tossed.
Our country's mood now needs to be
changing.

Support our Red slate
With me at its top.
Show up at the polls
Like a fall's bumper crop.
Then there's no way the Dems
Can bring our march to a stop.
We must show strength and that anger is
raging.
The fake media's drama
Will turn out a flop,
Once our country's mood is seen to be
changing.

Yes, the fake media's drama
Will turn out a flop,
Once our country's mood is seen to be
changing.

TRUMP SUPPORTERS
Make America strong again. Make America
great again! (Crescendo) Keep them out! Send
them back!! America for Americans!!!

> (TRUMP walks away from lectern,
> shaking hands with SUPPORTERS as
> AIDES and STAFF join him.)

TRUMP

You saw that? How they adore me? They love
hearing that the country has its troubles.
Makes them forget about their own. Gives
them something else to complain about. If I
tell them I'll solve the country's problems
then they'll feel I can solve theirs, too.
See? It's beautiful, perfect. That's how
we'll do it. A little fear in their hearts
is all we need.

> (TRUMP's advisor, **STEPHEN MILLER** - a
> lanky, balding man in an ill-fitting
> suit - comes forward.)

MILLER

That's good, Sir. Very good.

TRUMP

You like how I put that?

MILLER

Very much, Sir. That's worked before and we
can use that.

TRUMP

It's how I deal with bankers. They hate to
lose even more than they love to win.

MILLER

Exactly. Fear is a powerful motivator. If we
sell it right, that's all we need.

ACT ONE

MILLER
"ALL YOU NEED IS FEAR"

People feeling stressed is no surprise.
There's always some issue that will get
a rise.
It's never matters what is known,
It's about how they'd like it to be
shown,
And that's easy ...

We'll free their problems from the
Democrats' disguise.
Tell them what they've been told are
far Left's lies.
It doesn't matter what's true, you see,
It's all about naming an enemy,
And that's easy ...

All you need is fear.
All you need is fear.
All you need is fear, fear.
A little fear is all you need.

Everyone likes to think that what they
lack
Comes from what's been done behind
their back.
They'll boil to see they've paid for
what others got free,
And that's easy ...

ACT ONE

One good way to keep our Right on track
Is to make the case some slip in
through a crack.
Press for that wall, show how the Dems
are opposed to it all.
That'll make it easy ...

All you need is fear.
All you need is fear.
All you need is fear, fear.
A little fear is all you need.

There's always something a person holds
dear.
The trick then is to show that some
danger is near.
Your art of the deal was always to have
something important to sell.
Now that's fear, fear.
All you need is fear.

All you need is fear.
All you need is fear, fear.
Fear is all you need.
All you need is fear, fear.
A little fear is all you need.

> (Supporters enthusiastically surround
> MILLER.)

> (TRUMP nods, turns, acknowledges the
> continuing ovation, which suddenly
> ceases. His supporters become static.

ACT ONE

Action shifts to CLINTON and her
SUPPORTERS, who haven't heard
MILLER'S advice.)

CLINTON
(Addressing SUPPORTERS) He's really
something. You've got to wonder who writes
for him. Probably that Stephen Miller
character has a lot of input. Sounds like
him. It's a lesson in history, isn't it?

CLINTON SUPPORTER ONE
I'd say so. But that does it for him. Right?
Even the Republicans aren't going to buy
into all of that doom and gloom crap.

CLINTON SUPPORTER TWO
He's made it look like the country's poor,
in danger, and falling apart. Really? What
world does he live in? (Laughs) He's faker,
a charlatan, a media clown - exactly how
we've seen him on TV. We can't help but win
now.

CLINTON
Well, he does have a gift for rousing the
crowd.

CLINTON SUPPORTER ONE
Right. *His* crowd.

CLINTON
Trump could pose a problem for us, I'm
afraid.

CLINTON SUPPORTER TWO
Why? His kind of retro European populism
isn't going to play here. There aren't
enough who think like that. Times are good.
We're on the right side of that.

CLINTON

I wish I could believe that. We'll have to
make sure to control the way the debates go.

(CLINTON walks among her supporters,
smiling but then looking pensive.)

CLINTON
"DON'T BE SMUG TONIGHT"

I sense a bad mood is now building.
I sense Trump has found a voice.
I sense the center may be yielding.
I sense some will pick that choice.

Don't be smug tonight,
Just because you think we're right.
There's a bad mood on the rise.

Trump's good at making people waver,
To worry everything is going bad.
The main things that he has to offer
Are stories to make his supporters mad.

Don't be smug tonight,
Just because you think we're right.
There's a bad mood on the rise.

I feel the hot wind of emotion
Rising where once there was firm
thought.
I see a blight upon our nation
Sickening the roots for which we
fought.

ACT ONE

So don't be smug tonight,
Just because you think we're right.
There's a bad mood on the rise.

I fear the alt-Right and its hatred.
I fear they'll proudly march one day.
I fear the return of days thought long
dead.
I feel that Trump has found a way.

Don't be smug tonight,
Just because you think we're right.
There's a bad mood on the rise.

No, don't be smug tonight,
Just because you think we're right.
There's a bad mood on the rise.
Yes, a bad mood on the rise.

> (CLINTON and her SUPPORTERS drift
> close to monitors, become static.)

> (Action shift to TRUMP SUPPORTERS, in
> red shirts and red hats, emblazoned
> with MAGA, shaking placards and
> applauding as he speaks. TRUMP moves
> saccade-like from place to place, his
> high-light blinking off then on again
> as he assumes different positions
> across upstage left and center, but
> always looking down on the crowd.)

TRUMP
We'll make America great again!

ACT ONE

TRUMP SUPPORTERS
MAGA! MAGA!

TRUMP
(New position) America for Americans again.

TRUMP SUPPORTERS
Send 'em back! Send 'em back!

TRUMP
(New position) We need that wall and we'll build that wall!

TRUMP SUPPORTERS
Build that wall! Build that wall!

TRUMP
(New position) I'm the one, the only one.

> (TRUMP takes off his red MAGA hat and waves it about, beaming at his supporters.)

TRUMP SUPPORTERS
He's the one. He's the only one. God Bless Donald Trump!

> (TRUMP SUPPORTERS go silent, waving placards and hats while fixed in place.)

CLINTON SUPPORTERS IN A CLUSTER ABOUT CLINTON, STAGE RIGHT. TV MONITORS TAKEN OFF STAGE.

> (CLINTON SUPPORTERS turn to look at their counterparts and TRUMP.)

ACT ONE

CLINTON
It's really sad for the Republican Party.
They've allowed themselves to be bought. The
only reason he's running is to build his
business. Wait until they realize his
campaign is just a promo for himself and his
hotels.

CLINTON SUPPORTER TWO
He knows he's going to lose, but just
doesn't care. Look at him smile. He's having
fun!

CLINTON
Fun? I can't imagine this would be fun for
anyone. It's hard work.

CLINTON SUPPORTER ONE
Well, not for him, it seems. Right?

CLINTON
Let's see if it still seems that way when we
debate. It's a good thing he thinks he's
smart. He'll open so many doors, so many
lines of attack with his big mouth, his
little mind won't be able to cope.

CLINTON SUPPORTER TWO
That's a good one! We'll have to use that!

STAGE SET FOR THE DEBATE: TWO LECTERNS AT
CENTER; DESK AT RIGHT, WITH **MODERATORS ONE AND
TWO** BEHIND.

> (HILLARY CLINTON and TRUMP behind
> their respective lecterns, each doing
> their best to ignore the other.)

MODERATOR ONE
(As a continuation) ... The next question is
for Mister Trump. As you know, a tape of you

ACT ONE

has aired. Here's what's on it "When you're a star you can do anything. Grab them by the pussy. You can do anything," you said. What can you tell us about that?

TRUMP
Just talk. Buddy talk. Locker room talk, like men do. Nobody has more respect for women than Donald J. Trump.

CLINTON
(Looking at MODERATOR) He can claim that here, but it shows what he thinks about women, how he thinks he can treat women.

TRUMP
(Furious, pacing behind CLINTON) How about Bill Clinton, your husband and a failed president. There's never been anybody in the history of politics that's[sic] been so abusive to women.

CLINTON
(Into mic, calm and proud, but looking at TRUMP) I think it's clear to anyone who heard that video that it represents exactly who he is. I may have disagreed with prior Republican nominees for president but never questioned their fitness to serve.

TRUMP
Fitness? (Jabbing a finger at CLINTON) Using a private server when you were Secretary of State? Hiding emails from the public when you were doing the government's business shows how unfit YOU are! You should be ashamed of yourself.

ACT ONE

CLINTON
You've attacked immigrants, women, Muslims,
prisoners of war, liberals, scientists.... I
could go on and on. Exactly who are not
objectionable to you?

TRUMP
(Voice rising) I'll tell you what's
objectionable - having some one who's not
even legally allowed to be President having
been given the oath.

CLINTON
(To MODERATORS) She said it best: "When they
go low, we go high."

TRUMP
(Speaking away from the mic, as if only to
his supporters) Loser. Sad, sad losers.

CLINTON
You distrust foreigners, but you praise
Putin of Russia, who has directed attacks
upon our media. Never has a foreign power
worked so hard to influence our elections.

TRUMP
That's another Democrat hoax. Never
happened. I don't know Putin, but it never
happened.

MODERATOR TWO
Well, let's finish up with this: Would each
of you tell us one positive thing about the
other? Misses Clinton? You first.

CLINTON
(Throws back her head and laughs) I respect
his children.

ACT ONE

TRUMP
She's a fighter, and I consider that to be a
very good trait. Very good.

> (Lecterns and the two behind go off
> stage left. MODERATORS stand and talk
> privately.)

MODERATOR ONE
That wasn't particularly enlightening, I
must say. And became rather uncomfortable by
the end.

MODERATOR TWO
I agree. Donald Trump continues his race to
the bottom.

MODERATOR ONE
(Chuckles) So, you think he lost?

MODERATOR TWO
The debate? Possibly. But lose the election?
Perhaps not. We'll have to see how this
plays out. Either way, though, you can tell
he loves it.

MODERATOR ONE
He's rather like a pit bull - loves to bite
hard and hang on. That's his style. "When
they go high, go for the balls!" (Laughs)

MODERATOR TWO
Hope your mic is off. But yes, exactly.
(Laughing) With respect to another gender,
at any rate!... It's obvious he loves being
combative. And it's more exposure for his
brand. So win or lose, he wins. He's always
played a great game.

ACT ONE

MODERATOR ONE
That's his advantage. He's making it a game, a TV reality show, and have fun. His base eats it up. You can see it on their faces at his rallies. It's like a love affair!

MODERATOR TWO
Actually, more like a fan-fest, except with the middle-aged instead of teens.

MODERATOR ONE
(Chuckles) And being taken back to a past they never really lived.

MODERATOR TWO
But wish for, yes. I think you're exactly right. His people may not really hear what he's saying, but they're thrilled by him saying it.

MODERATOR ONE
Well, this would be fun for me, too, if I were sure he wasn't going to win.

MODERATOR TWO
I hope you're damn sure your mic is off.

MODERATOR ONE
It is.

MODERATOR TWO
Better double check! Just for fun.

MODERATOR ONE
Yes, ha ... Just for fun!

ACT ONE

MODERATORS, SINGLY AND IN UNISON
"TRUMP JUST WANTS TO HAVE FUN"

Trump smiles back at the adoring eyes.
His Party says that he's gone too far
with his lies.
But he's learned well since he's a
fortunate son,
And Trump, he's having much fun.
Trump just wants to have fun.

The questions flow after he picks each
fight.
The old Pols fear that he'll never get
his head right.
Old GOP, you know you're under the gun.
But Trump, he wants to have fun.

Trump just wants to have fun.
That's all he really wants.
Some fun.
When the campaign day is done,
Yes, Trump, he wants to have fun.
Trump just wants to have fun.

Some run with their dark bias and rage
Well hidden away, never brought up on
stage.
This guy wants his to know the light of
the sun.
Yes, Trump, he wants to have fun.
Trump just wants to have fun.

ACT ONE

That's all he really wants.
Some fun.
When the campaign day is done,
Yes, Trump, he wants to have fun.
Trump just wants to have fun.

He says if he can't get his own way,
He'll slander the vote as a sham and a
ploy.
Oh, Vladimir, we know you're his number
one.
Yes, Trump, he wants to have fun.

Trump just wants to have fun.
That's all he really wants.
Some fun.
When the campaign day is done,
Yes, Trump, he wants to have fun.

MODERATOR TWO
So true. So true. And they love him for it.
He could win!

MODERATOR ONE
Yes. What they love is his style. A true
media star! But is he really serious? You
think he can convince a majority?

MODERATOR TWO
Well, if he gets majorities in the right
states, he can. But I'm not sure he cares at
this point. Wouldn't surprise me if he
really *didn't* want to win. Watch him up
there. Don't listen so much to what he says;
watch how he says it. He's having fun!

MODERATOR ONE
You're probably right. His trick is to have his supporters NOT really listen, to just react and go with the sugar high. Like with donuts for breakfast!

MODERATORS (AS ABOVE)
That's all he really wants.
Some fun.
When the campaign days are done.
Yes, Trump, he'll want to have fun.
Trump always wants to have fun.

That's all he really wants,
Some fun.
When the campaign days are done.
When the campaign days are done, yes,
Trump, will want to have fun.
Trump always wants to have fun.

STAGE SLOWLY GOES DARK. UNDECIPHERABLE NEWS BROADCAST VOICES IN BACKGROUND.

END OF ACT ONE

ACT TWO

EMPTY STAGE, LIGHTS DIM. VOICES OFFSTAGE CAN
BE HEARD RECITING ELECTION RESULTS. SOME
CARRY A RISING TONE OF DISMAY, OTHERS JOYFUL.
IT'S VERY LATE ON ELECTION NIGHT. STAGE
LEFT: TRUMP SUPPORTERS (WITHOUT TRUMP),
STATIC. STAGE RIGHT: CLINTON AND HER
SUPPORTERS LIKEWISE STATIC.

OFFSTAGE MUSICAL REPRISE, IN TANDEM AND
OVERLAP:

TRUMP SUPPORTERS (EBULLIENT)
"TRUMP JUST WANTS TO HAVE FUN"

CLINTON SUPPORTERS (SUBDUED)
"DON'T BE SMUG TONIGHT"

VOICES OFF STAGE
Michigan? Really? What about Florida?

Wow, no one's laughing now. This's so sad,
so scary.

He got Pennsylvania, too!? Amazing! Looks
like the polls had it wrong!

Wisconsin - that makes it 538! He's won!!!

How did this happen? I can't believe it!

All the polls were so against him.

We fooled them ... for sure!

LIGHTS UP ON CLINTON CONTINGENT. CLINTON
STANDING ON AN ELEVATED PLATFORM.

ACT TWO

CLINTON

I want to thank you for your support and all your hard work. It's disappointing, I know. But the effort was worthwhile and I'm proud to have been here with you. I am proud that you were here with me. I hope you'll hold on to that and start thinking about twenty twenty.

CLINTON SUPPORTER

You, too, Hillary!

CLINTON

No. Sorry. This is it for me. For all of you, this is just another step, not the journey. But ... (She scans the crowd, her smile gradually fading.) but I am disappointed that I didn't do better for us, for the country. This is a very dark day, I'm afraid.

CLINTON
"SOMBER WEDNESDAY"

Somber Wednesday.

Wednesday's dawned fateful.
Last night was a cold caress.
Friends, strange dark shadows
Have spoiled our warm success.

Regrets and excuses
Will never undo this turn.
Only the future will
Offer a chance to relearn.

ACT TWO

Four years must go by
Before we can right this wrong.
Can we foresee voter remorse?
Or must we face a long sad song?

Somber, fateful Wednesday.

The election is over.
I've no desire to review it all.
My chance has gone,
I won't chase another fall.

Soon he'll take office
And strip away all our tools.
The people have spoken,
No point in saying they are fools.

Before I leave you all
It's important that I say,
Be true to our party's roots,
Twenty eighteen is not so far away.

Somber, bodeful Wednesday.

It's important that you strive
To put the darkness of this day behind.
You must be steadfast in our roots,
And keep twenty eighteen firmly in your
mind.

Bodeful, fateful Wednesday.

ACT TWO

CLINTON AND HER SUPPORTERS BECOME STATIC AS
THEIR LIGHTING DIMS.

ACTIVITY RESUMES FOR TRUMP SUPPORTERS. THEIR
LIGHTING BRIGHTENS.

> (TRUMP SUPPORTERS mill about with big
> smiles. Hugs and slaps on the back.)

TRUMP SUPPORTERS
"BOLD TRUMP"

Bold Trump!
You've made our hearts sing.
You've made being Red groovy.
Bold Trump!

Bold Trump,
You know we love you.
But we want to know it's sure.
So say it's OUR America once more.
We love you.

Bold Trump,
Your words have moved us.
Now we want to hear for sure.
Say you'll keep THEM far from our
shore.
Say THEY won't find an open door.

Bold Trump!
You've made our hearts sing.
You've made being Red groovy.
Bold Trump!

ACT TWO

Bold Trump,
Your plans have moved us.
You know it's for you we'll pray
As long as you'll make it pay!
We love you.

Bold Trump,
Your plans have roused us.
Now we want to hear you say
That the jobs'll be back one day,
That they'll be here to stay.

Bold Trump!
You've made our hearts sing.
You've made being Red groovy.
Bold Trump!
You've awakened us.
We love you!

"SOMBER WEDNESDAY" AND "BOLD TRUMP" REPEAT
WITH BOTH SIDES OVERLAPPING AS A CHAOTIC
CHORALE. STAGE SUDDENLY TO BLACK.

SILENT PAUSE.

STAGE DIM. TRUMP INAUGURATION DAY: SCENES OF
THE NATIONAL MALL, ONLOOKERS, AND DISMAL
WEATHER PROJECTED ON REAR WALL. "HAIL TO THE
CHIEF" MARCH BUILDS THEN FADES. EXCERPTS FROM
TRUMP'S INAUGURAL ADDRESS AT LOW VOLUME THEN
BUILDING. HOUSE SPEAKERS SET TO OUT OF PHASE,
SO SOURCE OF MUSIC AND WORDS IS OBSCURED.

TRUMP'S VOICE

(Softly) For too long a small group in our
nation's capital has reaped the rewards.

Politicians prospered, but the jobs left and
the factories closed. The establishment
protected itself but not the citizens of our
country.

(Louder) Today, January 20 2017, will be
remembered as the day the people became the
rulers of this nation again.

From this day onwards it is only going to be
America first - America first!

(Full volume) Together we will make America
strong again.

We will make America wealthy again.

We will make America safe again.

We will make America great again.

LIGHTS UP

> (TRUMP SUPPORTERS, casually dressed
> in a preponderance of red, drift in
> stage from right and left, most with
> MAGA hats.)

> (Scattered repetitions of "Make
> America Great Again" and "America
> First," etc.)

> (STEPHEN MILLER moves among
> SUPPORTERS, urging them on.)

ACT TWO

MILLER

He's your man! The one you wanted.

TRUMP SUPPORTERS

Donald Trump is our man! The one we want!

MILLER

Now, finally, you have a president who will
do something about the problems we face.

TRUMP SUPPORTERS

We want America to be great again!!!

(Supporters drift downstage, turning
to face audience in a single row.)

MILLER

It will be! You know where many of our
problems - crime and drug and jobs and
health care - have come from, don't you?
Immigration! It's only one of the issues
that have been neglected too long by the
Washington elites. But it's a good place to
start!

TRUMP SUPPORTERS

(To audience) Them. Yes, it's because of
them, the others. And we have no wall!

(Syncopated group speech) Where our children
go to school
The teachers all have their hands full
With new arrivals that won't speak English.

Their parents took our jobs, aren't taxed a
dime.
When out of work many turn to crime.
Well, at last we've a chance to get *our*
wish.

ACT TWO

It's not fair what has been done,
Openin' our borders to just anyone.
The only thing that'll save us now is to
keep out the trash!

Speak the truth, Donald, like it is!

TRUMP SUPPORTERS
"BUILD THAT WALL"

We don't need no immigration.
We don't need no for'ners at all.
No more elites sayin' we should make
room.
Democrats, leave that wall alone!
Hey! Rabble rousers! Let him build that
wall!
In the end, it'll be best to pay for
that wall.
Hear our voices, what we want is more
steel in that wall!

We don't want no immigration.
We don't want no for'ners at all.
No more Blues cryin' that we should
make room.
Democrats, leave that wall alone!

Hey! Rabble rousers! Let him build that
wall!
In the end, it'll be best to pay for
that wall.
Hear our voices, what we need are more
staves in that wall!

ACT TWO

(Loudly) The Dems got it wrong! Yes, say it,
Donald.
If you don't have a wall, how can you have a
country?
How can you have a country if you don't have
a wall?
Yeah, you! You tea sippin' libs. Pay for
that wall!

> We don't need no immigration.
> We don't need no for'ners at all.
> No more elites saying we should make
> room.
> Democrats! Leave that wall alone!

> Hey! Rabble rousers! Let Trump build us
> that wall!
> In the end, it'll be best just to pay
> for that wall.
> Hear our voices, what we lack are more
> miles of that wall!

> We don't need no immigration.
> We don't need no for'ners at all.
> No more elites sayin' we should make
> room.
> Democrats! Release the funds for that
> wall!

> > (TRUMP SUPPORTERS scatter and drift
> > off. Receding repeats ad lib: "You're
> > the one," "Build that wall," "Lead
> > us!" "You're OUR president!" etc.
> > MILLER scans audience with a flat
> > expression then exits.)

ACT TWO

STAGE DARK. SOUND BACK TO NORMAL. CURTAIN UP ON FESTIVE INAUGURAL BALL. MEN AND WOMEN IN FORMAL DRESS, MURMURING AND MINGLING.

ORCHESTRAL: "THE ARRIVAL OF THE QUEEN OF SHEBA" FROM HANDEL'S ORATORIO *SOLOMON*.

> (TRUMP sweeps into Convention Center, **MELANIA** on his arm, both in formal attire. Those in attendance applaud. TRUMP smiles, greets, and waves. MELANIA smiles. TRUMP goes to dais, picks up mic.)

ORCHESTRAL GIVES WAY TO FAINT STRAINS OF "MY WAY" OFFSTAGE.

TRUMP

I'm glad all of you are here. It was a very, very well attended Inaugural. A beautiful, beautiful event. So many were turned away. Even here, there were so many that[sic] wanted to come. Many more than we could accommodate. Too many, so many. Too bad, so sad. We'll have to celebrate ourselves without them. That's alright. Isn't it? (Applause)

TRUMP
"I'VE HAD FUN AND GAVE THEM PAIN"

*(Jovially)I woke up this morning aware
that I had won.*

*You know the Dems were sure of an end
to me.*

*At last my Right thinking friends can
bask in my sun.*

*I'll undo years of wrongs and rewrite
history.*

-54-

ACT TWO

I've had fun and gave them pain.
Now we'll have sunny days without end.
Few Republicans were counted on as
friends,
But they'll soon see what is rising up
again.

With you as my loyal base, I can work
at last to repair
A government that hasn't worked for you
at all.
First thing I'll do when I sit in that
chair
Is sign a law to get us that long
strong wall.

I've had fun and gave them pain.
Now you and I'll have sunny days
without end.
Few Republicans could be counted on as
friends,
But they will soon see what is rising
up again.

> (TRUMP leaves dais. He and MELANIA
> mingle with the crowd accepting their
> adoration.)

We control the Hill now. The Dems will
have no say.
We can start getting done what's long
overdue.

ACT TWO

*In business I've learned that you don't
waste a day.
So enjoy this, our evening, there will
be a lot to do.*

*I've had fun and given them pain.
Now you and I'll have sunny days
without end.
Despite that few Republicans showed up
as friends,
They will have to recognize what has
risen up again.*

*We'll be the envy of all the other
lands
When I make DC a business that finally
works for you.
Don't worry about your future. It will
be in good hands.
You can count on me doing what I said
I'd do.*

*I've had fun and gave them pain.
Now you and I will have sunny days
without end.
Despite the few Republicans that[sic]
showed up as friends,
They'll soon see what has risen up
again.*

ACT TWO

*Yes, they all soon will see what has
risen up again.
They all will acknowledge what has
risen up again.*

INSTRUMENTAL BUILDS: STRAINS OF "MY WAY"

> (TRUMP moves downstage, scans
> audience, smiles, waves, then begins
> a slow dance with MELANIA.)

SOUND OF THUNDER IN DISTANCE AS LIGHT ON TRUMP
AND MELANIA FADES. STAGE RIGHT, FEMALE **TRUMP
SUPPORTER,** IN MAGA HAT AND HEAVY WORN COAT
DAMP FROM THE RAIN, APPROACHES. SHE IS
OUTSIDE, LOOKING IN.

> (TRUMP SUPPORTER looks about with a
> mixture of curiosity, defiance, and
> anxiety, softly muttering while
> glancing up at the rain clouds.)

TRUMP SUPPORTER
They must be having a fine time in there. I
wish I could see. It must be sad for Melania
to have to see on the news all those nasty
things that woman has said about Donald.
She's just looking for money. It's terrible
when people do things like that just to hurt
a great man and try to run off with a few
bucks.

TRUMP SUPPORTER
"STORMY WEATHER"
*Can't see why they can't make this go
away.
Stormy weather.*

ACT TWO

That our man and she were together,
She keeps claimin' all the time.
All the time.

The Dems don't play fair.
They find malfeasance everywhere.
Stormy weather.

He's just a man who found fun here and
there.
Why all the bother?
Why make such a bother?

> (More TRUMP SUPPORTERS arrive and
> join in.)

Were he to go away,
We'd lose the man who represents us.
If he stayed away, we know the Blues
would overtake us.
All we can do's pray that he'll not
forsake us,
But beat them at the polls once more.

Can't see why they can't make this go
away.
Stormy weather.

So our man and she were together.
Why such fussin' all the time?
All the time.

ACT TWO

If he stayed away, we know the Blues
would overtake us.
All we can do's pray that he'll not
forsake us.
It's up to us to make sure he won't
forsake us.
We must beat them at the polls once
more.

Why or why can't they make her go away?
Stormy weather.
So our man and she were together.
Why fake fussin' all the time?
All the time.
Why such fake fussin' all the time?
All the time.

STAGE DARK.

LIGHTS UP ON TRUMP AND **REINCE PRIEBUS** IN OVAL
OFFICE, STAGE LEFT. SOUND OF OUTSIDE RAIN.

TRUMP
I told Rudy to have Cohen take care of it.

PRIEBUS
Is Cohen directly involved?

TRUMP
Michael's my lawyer, that's all. He's been
with me for a long, long time. He'll do a
beautiful, beautiful job. The best. He's
good at that, very good. It's in their
blood.

ACT TWO

PRIEBUS

But, Sir, did he deal directly with Daniels?
You need to be aware —

TRUMP

(Interrupting) I'm perfectly aware, John
It's about money. Money, money. That's all
it'll take to make it go away. It's just
another of the Democratic crowd's terrible,
terrible attempts to cause trouble. Her low-
life lawyer — who's probably working with
that third-rate politician, Pelosi — are
trying to make it into something, but it's
nothing. Nothing. Michael's a great guy. A
great, great negotiator. He'll deal with it.

PRIEBUS

Well, I would advise that —

TRUMP

Rudy kept watch and he'll keep watching,
John. Anything else?

FLASH THEN A CLAP OF THUNDER.

> (Both look out of oval office
> window.)

PRIEBUS

That was close.

TRUMP

(Picks up handset.) Hold them for a minute
then send them in. (To PRIEBUS) It's Rudy.
Anything else? No? (Motions for PRIEBUS to
leave.)

> (**RUDY GIULIANI** enters, **MICHAEL COHEN**
> following. GIULIANI gives TRUMP a big
> smile.)

ACT TWO

TRUMP

You're wet, Michael. No umbrella? Not too
smart, in this weather. Look at Rudy. He's
dry as a bone.

GIULIANI

I always plan ahead, Mister President.

TRUMP

Well? Are we done?

COHEN

All well done, Sir. Signed and sealed.
(Reaches into jacket inner pocket.)

> (GIULIANI sits. COHEN remains
> standing.)

GIULIANI

Leave it. I'll get it from you later. (To
TRUMP) You don't need to know anything about
it, except that it's done. And done pretty
cheaply, all things considered. Good thing
she's just a —

TRUMP

(Interrupting) I don't need to hear that,
Rudy. Everybody knows that. Everybody. All I
want to hear is that it's been taken care
of. (Motions to COHEN) Yes, he's a great
guy. Michael's a creative, incredible guy.
(To COHEN) You're my guy, Michael.

COHEN

Thank you, Sir. It's my honor to serve. I've
learned from you, Mister President. The art
of the deal: Make it quick, irresistible,
and final.

> (COHEN paces back and forth.)

ACT TWO

COHEN
"DIRTY DEAL"

When you're having trouble with your
fun filled past,
Like a ho' was giving you a pain.
You wanted to move on; it wasn't meant
to last.
But she was trying to make a stain.

I responded to your call.
It was I who jumped on the ball,
Because there was something to be done.
You just needed to phone,
Punch up Mike Cohen,
Your faithful hired gun.

Dirty deal, done real quick.
Dirty deal, done real quick.
(Dirty deals and they're done real
quick.)
(Dirty deals and they're done real
quick.)

When you've got a lady with a lawyer
who's a creep,
But he's a master at his game.
You didn't need to worry, didn't need
to lose any sleep.
I'm even better at the same.

ACT TWO

You punched up that phone,
Called on Mike Cohen.
I answer night and day.
You wrote me a check,
So I could stack the deck,
And make them glad to slink away.

Dirty deal, done real quick.
Dirty deal, done real quick.
(Dirty deals and they're done real
quick.)
(Dirty deals and they're done real
quick.)

I'm loyal to you, to your business and
your son.
So don't think twice, don't have a
care,
I'm ready when any deals need to be
done.
Think about our past. You'll know that
I'll be there.

Pay me the fee, I'm happy to be
Your super-silent bag man.
Just pick up the phone,
You'll not be alone.
Trust me. You know you can.

ACT TWO

Dirty deal, done real quick.
(Dirty deals and they're done real
quick.)
Dirty deal, done real quick.
(Dirty deals and they're done real
quick.)
Dirty deal, done real quick.
(Dirty deals and they're done real
quick.)

Just pick up the phone,
You'll not be alone.
Please trust me. You know you can.
Dirty deals, done real quick.

TRUMP
Thank you, Mike. Keep Rudy up to date, but I
hope this's the end of that.

> (TRUMP nods to COHEN, who stands for
> a moment then leaves.)

We've got to get my administration up to
speed, Rudy. Full speed. I want to do great
things. Beautiful, beautiful things. That
Democratic House crowd is like a bunch of
dogs after a bone - trying to get something
that's not there, foaming at the mouth. I
need to shut them up. The fake media, too. I
want to show them who's boss, do something
big. (Into intercom.) Have Priebus come in.
(To GIULIANI) I think you'd better go, Rudy.

> (GIULIANI leaves, nodding to PRIEBUS
> in passing, which is not
> acknowledged.)

ACT TWO

SHIFT TO WHITE HOUSE CANDLELIGHT DINNER MID-SEPTEMBER, 2017. TRUMP AND MELANIA WITH GUESTS AT HEAD TABLE. HE RISES, STRIDES TO DAIS TO ADDRESS OTHER GUESTS, MIMES SPEAKING FOR A FEW MINUTES - ARMS ACTIVE - THEN CONCLUDES:

TRUMP
... Now I'm going to turn it over to the star of the Trump family. They love her out there. After the Hurricane Irma, we walked all over Florida. After Harvey, we walked all over Texas, and they're loving Melania. They certainly love her out there.

> (Applause. MELANIA takes her place at the podium, accepting a light kiss on the cheek from TRUMP)

MELANIA
(Smiles) I have seen the true spirit of this country, an unwavering commitment to overcome. And you are his loyal supporters.... He thanks you and wants you to know he's dedicated to fighting your battle. And, of course, I thank you. I thank you for him and for myself.... Yes, he's just a man, but he's a great man. (Points to her husband.) A hardworking, brilliant man who needs your support.

MELANIA
"SMEAR'S THE NATURE OF THEIR GAME"
(Warmly) Please let me tell you a thing or two
About this man who has wealth and taste.
He's vowed to make us strong again
And has not a second to waste.

ACT TWO

He was there when the Towers came down
And saw what it meant to be weak.
He vowed then to put an end to it
And make terrorists sweat and quake.

He's here because of you.
I hope you'll grow his fame.
Don't let his enemies weigh on you.
Smear's the nature of their game.

With our government full of shifty
fools,
He saw that we needed sharp change.
He's worked hard at this for many long
years.
That elites are upset isn't strange.

Yes, he's here because of you.
I hope you'll grow his fame.
Don't let his enemies get to you,
Smear's the nature of their game.

He promised a wall and build it he
will,
If Congress will get out of his way.
"America First" is his number one job.
He's right that only the worthy should
stay.

ACT TWO

He's returning jobs to the U S A,
Something that he long promised he'd
get done.
He's standing up to China's misdeeds,
And needs strong support from everyone.

He's here because of you.
I hope you'll grow his fame.
Don't let his enemies discourage you.
Smear's the nature of their game.

Young American men are trained and sent
far away
To fight where there's no hope of gain.
Those Mideast wars go on and on,
While we watch with despair and pain.
He'll work hard and his best will be
great.
He'll make our America work for you.
He'll make our America proud again.
I stand with him and I hope you will
too.

You'll watch with glee,
While the liberals flee
From the decades of mess that they've
made.

ACT TWO

He's here because of you.
I hope you'll grow his fame.
Don't let his enemies influence you,
Smear's the nature of their game.

Yes, you'll watch with glee,
While the liberals flee
From the decades of mess that they've
made.

He's only here because of you.
I know you'll grow his fame.
Don't let his enemies trouble you,
Smear's the nature of their game.

STAGE DARK.

OVAL OFFICE. DOOR CLOSING AS IF SOMEONE HAS
JUST LEFT THE ROOM. TRUMP, ALONE, FACES TV.

> (TRUMP looks at his wrist. Annoyed,
> he throws a thick stack of briefing
> papers onto his desk. He points
> remote at TV.)

TRUMP
Lindsey said he'd be on today.... I should
watch. He's finally turned himself around.

TRUMP'S TV BECOMES THE SET OF FOX NEWS, WITH
LINDSEY GRAHAM SITTING WITH A NUMBER OF
COMMENTATORS, **FOX FRIENDS**. HE IS IN THE MIDDLE
OF A MONOLOGUE, CAMERAS FACING HIM.

ACT TWO

GRAHAM

... but put all that aside. The Democrats
are scheming to make a case where there is
no case. It's that simple. They're trying to
make the President look bad but it's only a
reflection of their own ineptitude, of their
vicious, unprincipled, unjustified —
unjustifiable actually — attacks. Donald
Trump is, in fact, probably the best
president we've ever had. He's far sighted
and he's strong. He's exactly what this
country needs for a change - someone
principled and strong.

GRAHAM
"PRESCIENT, POTENT PRESIDENT"

(Rapid tempo.)
Trump proffers a perfect portrait of a
prescient, potent President.
He's skilled in matters of our world
and how to run a government.

> (GRAHAM glances at FOX FRIENDS across
> from him, then gets up and goes
> downstage to face audience.)

In science, both experimental and the
theoretical,
There are but few who know what he's
found clear; he's never antithetical.
If you're talking physics then Steven
Hawkin is the one to see.
Though Trump can say Schrodinger's cat
for him holds little mystery.

ACT TWO

As for climate change, he knows more
than a pack of spectacled PhDs.
And when it comes to black holes, you
must admit the most adept is he.

Trump has no time for books, you see,
but creates a steady stream of tweets.
And there's none, as he has said, who's
better in between the sheets.
In short, in matters of our world and
how to run a government,
He proffers a perfect portrait of a
prescient, potent President.

FOX FRIENDS

In short, in matters of our world and
how to run a government,
Trump proffers a perfect portrait of a
prescient, potent President.

    (GRAHAM moves to one side of stage,
    still addressing audience.)

GRAHAM

Trump knows the people's anomie and
extracts from it encomia.
He drives his foes to agony and basks
in friends' euphoria.
Conservatives do need a voice. Once
Buckley, now it's me you see!
The Far Right also craves a face. By
word and deed that's surely he.

ACT TWO

*Though in building towers he's highly
skilled, in politics he's not astute.
While some declaim this is a fault, he
knows what works and what is moot.
In economics he has few friends but, as
we see, can say a lot.
Friedmanian, Keynesian, to stir his
crowd these matter not.*

*His grasp of Giffen/Veblen goods is
innate not academic.
To get things done he needs no tome, he
relies upon polemic.
In short, in matters of our world and
how to run a government,
He proffers a perfect portrait of a
prescient, potent President.*

FOX FRIENDS

*In short, in matters of our world and
how to run a government,
Trump proffers a perfect portrait of a
prescient, potent President.*

GRAHAM

*Of military matters Trump knows more
than any medaled man.
He'll not seek to admit a wrong like
some contrite de Leguizamón.*

ACT TWO

*With allies of the West and East he's
prone to play it fast and loose.
Without a blush he's made it plain he
does not like that they're obtuse.
Except for terror aimed at us, he has
no brief for Muslim lore.
The Shia Sunni endless feud is ranked
by him a total bore.
Except for oil's strategic lure, he'd
have them fight till all are dead,
Like an ouroboros in ancient texts, be
self-consumed from tail to head!*

*His need for love is like most men's
but more acute, more active.
If to be defined by a single word he
would much prefer amative.
In short, in matters of our world and
how to run a government,
He proffers a perfect portrait of a
prescient, potent President.*

FOX FRIENDS
*In short, in matters of our world and
how to run a government,
Trump proffers a perfect portrait of a
prescient, potent President.*

(GRAHAM takes his seat.)

ACT TWO

GRAHAM AND FOX FRIENDS

*In short, in matters of our world and
how to run a government,
Trump proffers a perfect portrait of a
prescient, potent President.*

FOX FRIEND

Thank you, Senator. I believe you've covered
that very well. (To audience) After this
break for our sponsors, we'll have excerpts
from our recent exciting conversation with
Milo Hanrahan, the former editor of
Breitbart. You may know him better as Milo
Yiannopoulos. We'll be right back. (Smiles
into camera)

STAGE DARK

PRESIDENTIAL DESK HIGH-LIGHTED AT STAGE LEFT.
FLAGS ON EITHER SIDE, WINDOW OF OVAL OFFICE
BEHIND. TRUMP AT HIS DESK, STARING AT TV
SCREEN. **JARED KUSHNER** ENTERS AND TAKES A
CHAIR.

TRUMP

Good, good. I've got a lot for you to do,
Jared. All very important items to me. Very
important. You can be a big, big help. An
enormous help. I wish I had a son like you.
But you married my daughter; that's close
enough. Now, make me happy and make Ivanka
happy. There's a lot to get done.

KUSHNER

Thank you, Sir. Leave it to me. I'll get it
done for you.

ACT TWO

TRUMP

I have to get the Mideast under control,
Jared, to solve that Israeli-Palestinian
issue. Big issue, big issue. That'll boost
my popularity amongst your people, with
everyone, everyone. And drugs. The opioid
crisis is another terrible problem that the
do-nothing Democrats have just let fester.
The same goes for crime in general. How it's
been handled is so poor. Bad, very bad. The
entire government is out of control, not
working the way it should.

KUSHNER

Yes, Sir. I've been looking into all that.
You've given me an opportunity and I won't
waste it. You can count on me. I have a
number of ideas about how to get those done.

KUSHNER
"IT'LL BE SIMPLE"

It'll be simple to get things done.
Mid-East peace is only one.
People may say I don't know enough,
That the problems we face are just too
tough.

But seems simple.
(So simple. Yes, so simple.)
Looks very simple.
(So simple. Yes, so simple.)
Yes, it'll be simple.
(So simple. Yes, so simple.)
There's much to change; all is within
my range.

ACT TWO

I'm glad to hear that I'm your favorite
son.
That'll make it easy to get things
done.
The opioid curse has stained our towns
And Mexican drugs are all around.

That seems simple.
(So simple. Yes, so simple.)
Looks very simple.
(So simple. Yes, so simple.)
Yes, it'll be simple.
(So simple. Yes, so simple.)
There's much to change and that's
within my range.

It'll be simple to put things right.
Unfair trade is yet another fight.
Our Veterans get care below the norm,
And criminal justice badly needs
reform.

(KUSHNER gets up, approaches desk.)

All seems simple.
(So simple. Yes, so simple.)
Looks very simple.
(So simple. Yes, so simple.)
Yes, it'll be simple.
(So simple. Yes, so simple.)
There's much to change; all that's
within my range.

ACT TWO

It'll be simple to get things done.
I'm glad you agree that I'm the one.
Our government's been so badly run,
It's also past time to get that done.

Change seems simple.
(So simple. Yes, so simple.)
Looks very simple.
(So simple. Yes, so simple.)
Yes, it'll be simple.
(So simple. Yes, so simple.)
There's much to change; all fall within
my range.

      (KUSHNER moves to side of desk
      nearest door.)

It'll be simple to get things done.
I'm glad you feel that I'm the one.
Seems simple.
(So simple. Yes, so simple.)

Looks very simple.
(So simple. Yes, so simple.)
Yes, it'll be simple.
Trust me, it'll be simple.
(So simple. Yes, so simple.)
There's much to change; nothing is
beyond my range.
It'll be simple to get those done.
It'll be so simple to get things done.

ACT TWO

TRUMP

Fine, Jared. That's fine. Keep me informed.
(Desk phone beeps. He picks up handset as
KUSHNER leaves.) Have him come in.

    (GIULIANI enters, giving TRUMP a big
    smile.)

TRUMP

Rudy. How about those people, all those
wonderful, wonderful people at my rallies.
They love me!

GIULIANI

That's certainly correct. Huge crowds. (Big
smile) You need to keep doing that, keep the
excitement level up. We all love you....
Mister President, we have a problem,
however. That special —

TRUMP

Certainly. I'm the most loved President,
despite all that fake reporting. Those media
people never tell it straight. They're among
the most dishonest beings on Earth. It's
terrible, terrible, to have people like that
trying to screw me and mislead the people.
It's a good thing we still have at least one
honest network telling it straight. I'm the
most loved President ever. Everyone sees
that. Isn't that right, Rudy?

BACKGROUND MUSIC, "RUSSIAN DANCE" FROM
TCHAIKOVSKY'S *NUTCRACKER*. MUSIC STARTS SOFTLY
AND BUILDS SLOWLY, MOVING FROM STAGE RIGHT TO
LEFT.

GIULIANI

Of course, Mister President. The most ever
there was. (His big smile fades) But we have
a problem. Robert Mueller, the special

ACT TWO

counsel that Rod Rosenstein appointed, is digging into this Russian nonsense.

TRUMP
More of that again? That hoax? That Mueller's a closet Democrat, I'm sure. A Never Trumper, probably.

GIULIANI
He's a Republican actually. Worked under Bush, both of them. But Obama as well.

TRUMP
I knew it.

GIULIANI
He's pretty much an old school lawyer. Conservative. A straight ahead type of guy.

TCHAIKOVSKY BACKGROUND MUSIC, NOW FULLY STAGE LEFT, STOPS IN MID-PHRASE.

TRUMP
That Goddamned Sessions. It's all his fault. He ran off like a little boy, a baby. Ran off to hide and let this happen when I needed him. (Slumping in chair) It's the end of my presidency. I'm fucked.

GIULIANI
No need to be so glum, Mister President. It'll be just more of the Democrats' playing to the press, trying to get at you, to weaken you. It's for the benefit of their leftist crowd. A witch hunt. I know that game.

(TRUMP stands, moves around desk to GIULIANI.)

ACT TWO

TRUMP

A witch hunt. Exactly. Perfect, perfect
description. Well, I'll fight the bastards.
To hell with them.... I'll need your help,
Rudy. I need you to stand with me. Will you
do that? Can I count on you?

TRUMP
"STAND WITH ME, RUDY"

Now the time is here,
It's their plan from early this year,
To make a hoax all that people will
see.
But I won't give an inch,
Not a single, god-damned inch
For as long as you'll stand,
Stand with me.

Oh, Rudy, Rudy,
Stand with me. Yes, stand with me.
Just stand, please stand,
Stand with me.

With news that is fake,
The Dems will try to retake
What they lost in November to me.
But they won't, no they won't.
No, they can't, no they can't,
Not as long as you stand,
Stand with me.

ACT TWO

Oh, Rudy, Rudy,
Stand with me. Yes, stand with me.
Just stand, please stand,
Stand with me.

Rudy, Rudy,
Stand with me. Please stand with me.
Stand strong now and fight with me.
Fight with me.
Fight trouble with more trouble.
Don't you see?
Just stand with me.
Will you stand with me?
Stand and fight with me?

Oh, Rudy, Rudy,
Stand with me. Yes, stand with me.
Just stand, please stand,
Stand with me.

GIULIANI
You can count on that, Mister President.
I'll be there, I'll be everywhere for you.

TRUMP
They're going to put out all kinds of
stories to make me look bad. Dig up all
kinds of old rumors and fake facts.

GIULIANI
Don't worry, Mister President. Facts are
only true if you admit to them.

ACT TWO

TRUMP

Like that phoney climate change, that fake
science.

GIULIANI

Exactly, Mister President. Truth isn't
truth! Don't argue with facts; just dismiss
them.

(Giuliani stands next to his
President.)

TRUMP AND GIULIANI DUET:
TRUMP -/

Oh, Rudy, Rudy,
Stand with me. Yes, stand with me.
Just stand, please stand,
Stand with me.

Rudy, Rudy
Stand with me. Please stand with me.
Stand tall now and fight with me.
Fight with me.
Fight trouble with more trouble.
Don't you see? Just stand with me.
Stand with me.
Will you stand,
Stand and fight with me?

GIULIANI -/

Yes, Mister President,
I'll stand with you, stand with you.
I will stand, yes stand,
Stand with you.

ACT TWO

My Mister President,
I'll stand with you, yes, stand with
you,
Stand tall, and fight for you.
Fight for you.
I'll fight trouble with more trouble,
You'll see. Yes, you'll see.
Yes, you'll see.
You can count,
Rely and count on me.

-// END OF DUET

TRUMP
Thank you, Rudy. I feel better now. I've got
so much to do. Big plans. Historic plans.
Can't let people take advantage or get in
the way. So, do what you need to do. Get
right at it, like you did with that Daniels'
business.

GIULIANI
Cohen was front and center on that, Mister
President. I just helped it along.

(Both take their respective seats.)

TRUMP
Well, keep "helping things along," Rudy.
Rumors and hoaxes shouldn't be allowed to
get in the way. It's treasonous, treasonous.
Go wherever you need to go to keep the
traitor Democrats off balance. Especially
that Joe Biden clown. See if you can't get
something to slow him down. He and his son
were doing some bad, bad things in the
Ukraine, I understand. See what you can find

ACT TWO

out about that. We might need it for my
reelection campaign, if he lives that long.

GIULIANI
Yes, Sir, Mister President. I've been
looking into that. I believe I can get what
you need.

TRUMP
Good, good. I've got such a great mind and
unmatched wisdom, I can't let them — that
pack of clowns, those Democrats — get in the
way. I like how some of those other leaders
have it. Xi in China, for example. President
for life. That's much better for everyone,
when you have a smart leader that[sic]
people sit up for and listen to. Much better
for everyone. The country is much, much
better for it. They'll demand it when they
see whatever loser the Democrats put up.

GIULIANI
That's not our system, Mister President.

TRUMP
It needs to be. It should be, when you have
a great leader like me. The best the
country's seen. How often does that happen?
Not often. Not often.

> (TRUMP rises, moves close to flag,
> embraces it. GIULIANI leaves.)

TRUMP ISOLATED, HIGHLIGHTING FADES TO OFF.

OVAL OFFICE WEEKS LATER. TRUMP, SITTING AT
DESK, TALKING INTO HANDSET.

TRUMP
Yes. Well, it's their own fault. They
weren't smart enough. They didn't follow my

advice and ran terrible, terrible campaigns.
(Replaces handset)

VOICE FROM INTERCOM
General Kelly is here, Mister President.

TRUMP
(Pauses) Alright. (Pauses again) Send him
in.

      (**GENERAL KELLY** enters in civilian
      clothes. He holds out a folded
      newspaper.)

KELLY
Good morning, Sir. I'm sure you've seen the
mid-term results.

TRUMP
Yes. Terrible, yes. I watched on Fox. The
damn Democrats have managed a majority in
the House. We should have been able to
prevent that, General. Don't you think? That
was perfectly preventable.

      (GENERAL KELLY takes a seat without
      being asked. TRUMP notices, but says
      nothing.)

KELLY
Well, there were some who just didn't run an
effective campaign, Sir. It was close in
many cases, but not close enough for
recounts. We'll have to educate better in
twenty twenty.

TRUMP
Now I suppose that Russia hoax, that
disgusting witch hunt, will get even more
media time now. They'll scurry around making

sure of that. Them[sic] and their fake media
allies. Like a rat's nest of traitors.

KELLY
Possibly, Sir. Yes.... Pelosi will be the
new House speaker. We need to —

TRUMP
Of course, Pelosi'll be their speaker. A
fine pick. A fine, fine pick from the far
Left. I know all about her. She been one of
those nasty, nasty hoaxers from the start. A
second-rate politician. No, not second-rate
... probably third-rate. Crazy, nervous
Nancy.

KELLY
We can't change the mid-term results, Sir.
So we'll have to work with them, until we
can turn it around in the next election.

TRUMP
How can you work with crazy people like
that, General? Are you a closet Democrat
too? She and her head clown, Schumer, are
against everything I've promised. Working
with them is going to be very, very
difficult. Don't you see that? We have to
overcome them, not work with them.

KELLY
We can do both, Sir, if we must.

TRUMP
It all goes back to those crooked pollsters.
They were shouting we'd lose the House
before it even happened. They were wishing
for it. Everyone sees that. Everyone. Did
their best to make people think that way so
they wouldn't come out strong for our people

the way they should have. They're the real enemy you know, those biased media people. It's a stain on our country. It's a stain on democracy.

> (TRUMP rises and walks to window, looks out.)

TRUMP
"I SAW IT IN THE FAKE TIMES"

Oh, even Fox news said they knew
That the House was turning Blue.
We had guys who ran a lousy race,
A sad fact we'll just have to face.
Still, it hurt like hell that day
When Fox Friends said what they had to say.

But you saw, it was touted in the fake Times,
That the House was not to stay mine.
And now it's headlines in the fake Times,
No longer will the House be mine.

> (TRUMP smooths and straightens his overly long tie.)

When my Fox buds said they knew
That the house would be turning Blue,
I hated to believe what they had to say,
That they thought it wouldn't go my way.

ACT TWO

But our people showed too little
smarts.
They were clinging to their feel-good
charts.

Yes, despite the costly campaign line,
The House will no longer be mine.
Now it's headlines in the fake Times,
That no longer is the House mine.

Fake news clowns spend their time
Repeating the Dems sleazy party line.
They can't stand what I have to say,
But I'll keep saying it anyway.
No matter if what I'm telling you
Isn't absolutely, absolutely true,
The DC scene is just a big, big show,
That's all our core people need know.

Still, it's headlines in the fake
Times,
No longer is the House mine.
Yes, it was touted in the fake Times,
That the House was not to stay mine.
Now it's headlines in the fake Times,
No longer is the House mine.

Democrats were enraged that I won the
race.
It was Hillary they pictured in my
place.

ACT TWO

They made it clear from my
administration's start
They'd obstruct and play the spoiler's
part.
They plant stories that are total lies
And do everything we should despise.
The results are headlines in the fake
Times
That the House will no longer be mine.

Yes, it's bold headlines in the fake
Times
They're happy no longer is the House
mine.

Yes, it was touted in the fake Times,
That the House was not to stay mine.
Now it's headlines in the fake Times,
No longer is the House mine.

TRUMP

(Darkly) It's going to be harder, now, to push my agenda through. Much, much harder. The Dems' will make it much harder for the country, and the fake media's to blame. And so is having people, on my staff that[sic] aren't one hundred per cent loyal. That doesn't help, doesn't help at all.

     (TRUMP goes behind his desk and sits)

It's treasonous, General. You understand what I'm saying? I get a lot more information than you might think. From networks besides Fox, too, on occasion. And

ACT TWO

I hear what's being said around here. I need
more people that[sic] will help and fewer
that won't, fewer that[sic] are negative.
That'll be all for now, General.

(GENERAL KELLY stands, stares at
TRUMP for a moment then leaves.)

OVAL OFFICE SOME TIME LATER.

(TRUMP speaking with his new chief of
staff, **JOHN "MICK" MULVANEY**)

TRUMP
I'm glad to have finally gotten Kelly out of
here. He was never on my side. Never. I'll
need you, Mick, to make up for lost time.

MULVANEY
I'm ready, Sir.

TRUMP
First thing is, I want to use this budget
bill to get that wall funded. I have to get
that wall funded.

MULVANEY
It'll take some arm twisting. But I believe
we can get that done.

TRUMP
I suppose we'll have to get Pelosi and her
cronies in here. Got to get that wall up - a
strong and beautiful wall - as quickly as we
can, before I sign any spending bill. Quite
a Christmas present the Democrats given the
American people — a government shutdown!

MULVANEY
I'll arrange for a meeting, for here at the
White House. Get the House and the Senate

Democratic leads in here. It will make for good optics. Show you're trying to work it out.

TRUMP
Do it soon. I don't want this shutdown to need to go on much longer.

MULVANEY
Yes, Sir. Right after Congress gets back. First thing in January.

STAGE DARK. FAINT MUSICAL STRAINS OF "MY WAY"

OPEN ON SPEAKER **NANCY PELOSI** IN HOUSE HALLWAY, STANDING BEFORE A CLUSTER OF MICROPHONES AND FACING A GROUP OF **REPORTERS**.

PELOSI
Senator Schumer and I have just met with the President about finalizing the budget and reopening the government. Unfortunately, Mister Trump called our meeting a "total waste of time."

REPORTER
What else can you tell us about your meeting with the President? Is it true he stormed out?

PELOSI
The main thing I can tell you is that he insists on making border security the primary issue. But have I not been clear on the wall? He demands that we pay for his wall. That's not the way our government works. We must negotiate, compromise, find common ground. That is what this President does not seem to get. It's not helpful to be petulant and say, "Well, we've got nothing

ACT TWO

to discuss," then walk out. However, we'll get past this and put the government back to work. We'll meet again.

PELOSI
"WE'LL MEET AGAIN"

We'll meet again.
Don't know where,
Don't know when.
But I'm sure we'll meet again and find
a way.
We'll work it through
Like democracies should do.
He'll compromise once he sees that it
will pay.

So, I want you to know
That we won't let it go.
I promise, it won't be long
Before the shutdown is through.
Just do what you should do,
And take your cue from this song.

We must meet again.
Don't know where,
Don't know when.
But I'm sure we'll meet again and find
a way.

REPORTERS

They'll meet again.
Don't know where,
Don't know when.

ACT TWO

But she's sure they'll meet again and
find a way.

They'll work it through
Like democracies must do.
Compromise will thrive once Trump sees
it will pay.

She wants us to know
And have us say that it's so,
That it won't be too long
Before the shutdown is through.
We must do as we should do.
And take our cue from this song.

PELOSI (AND REPORTERS)
We'll (They'll) meet again.
Don't know where,
Don't know when.
But I'm (she's) sure we'll (they'll)
meet again and find a way.

Yes, we'll (they'll) meet again.
Don't know where,
Don't know when.
I'm (She's) sure we'll (they'll) meet
again and find a way.

SLOW FADE.

END OF ACT TWO

ACT THREE

OVAL OFFICE, EARLY 2019. TRUMP MEETING WITH CHIEF OF STAFF, MICK MULVANEY. BOTH ARE SEATED.

TRUMP

We need to get past that Pelosi nag. She's a bigger clown than that Schumer. Always baiting the media and making us waste so much time on nothing, nothing. All this Russian nonsense — it's pure bullshit. Everybody knows that. Everybody. Mueller said it: No obstruction; no collusion. It's a delusion. The collusion delusion. That's so true, so true. But the House Democrats won't let it go! All because of that third-rate Pelosi, her gang of closed-door politicians, and their witch hunt. I want to get something concrete in the news. Do something big for our side.

MULVANEY

What do you have in mind, Sir?

TRUMP

I want a face-to-face with Putin. Have him say he never interfered. I'll get the little guy to make concessions and show the world how I'm in control. Not the other way around, like those traitors in Congress and the media keep saying.

MULVANEY

That would pose some difficulties, Mister President. For obvious reasons.

ACT THREE

TRUMP
Difficulties can always be managed. That's
why I have staff. I understand Putin. We get
on well. I can manage him. So let's get that
meeting.

MULVANEY
We'll have to prepare our desired endpoints.
He is a very slippery sort. He's in total
control over there. He's accustomed to
making things go his way.

> (TRUMP stands, MULVANEY follows
> suit.)

TRUMP
Fine, fine. Our meetings in Europe went
very, very well. I got along great with him
and he told me they had nothing to do with
messing with our election. More
important[sic], much more important, is that
we like each other. That was easy to see
when we met. We had nice long talks. We
understand each other very, very well. A
face-to-face would be a good media moment,
something to stick in the eyes of that Fake
Press corps.

MULVANEY
He's a very experienced negotiator also,
Mister President. We'll need to —

TRUMP
(Sideways) I understand him. I can handle
him. He respects business. And I know
business. I negotiate better than anyone,
certainly better than Putin.

> (TRUMP faces MULVANEY directly.)

TRUMP
"I'LL HANDLE HIM" (PUTIN)

Yes, you've told me. Sure, you've told me
That Putin is no damn fool.
He plays games like Soviet dames,
Except uses conflict as his tool.
And now the boys at our FBI
Claim Russia's been corrupting our polls.
Some yell that it's just like a war
The way they use Facebook trolls.

But Putin's my friend.
Yes, Vova's my friend.
He just enjoys being feared.
I'll handle him; I'll handle him.
I'll make a deal with him
And not give a thing away.
I'll handle him; I'll handle him.
I'll make a deal with him
And not give a thing away.

MULVANEY

Putin's agenda is clear, Mister President. He has time. And he doesn't have to worry about getting approval from anyone. Perhaps it would be better to focus first on reigning in North Korea?

TRUMP

Yes, good point, Mick. Getting that North Korea business settled would be a good thing, too. (Pacing) Yes, getting Kim to

agree on ending his nuclear and missile
tests, for example, would be good. A very,
very good thing to shut both Pelosi and the
Fake Media up.

MULVANEY
We'd have to be careful that Kim doesn't
turn any negotiations into a media circus.
Mainly, he wants attention on the world
stage. We've seen he's unpredictable and can
be vicious. It's best to keep in mind that —

TRUMP
"I'LL HANDLE HIM" (KIM)
*Mick, you've told me. Sure you've told
me*
That Kim has a nasty streak.
But I'm sure that he'll see it my way.
I'll have him give and not look weak.
His country's poor and on the edge.
He'll need us in the end.
I know he wants to stay on top,
So there's no doubt he will bend.

Oh, Kim is my friend.
Yes, Jong-Un is my friend,
He's just a little small and weird.
I'll handle him; I'll handle him.
I'll take a seat with him
And make a peace in our day.
I'll handle him; I'll handle him.
I'll take a seat with him
And make a peace in our day.

ACT THREE

TRUMP

Our last meeting was good. Very, very good.
Kim will lap it up like a puppy if I put him
in the spotlight again. He'll do whatever I
want.

MULVANEY

Realistically, Mister President, Kim Jong-Un
takes being Supreme Leader very seriously.
And he takes his missile and nuclear
capabilities, as objectively questionable as
they are, very seriously. He knows he can't
win but also knows he can give a nasty bite.
That might be all the advantage he feels he
needs.

TRUMP

I understand him. He expects to be leader
for life. Too bad Kim is not anything like
Xi or me. Too young. Too inexperienced.
Still, it will be good for us to meet face
to face. I'll negotiate a deal with him to
back away from the threats and name calling.
Get him to want what we could do for him,
the doors we could reopen for him. He's
ambitious. We understand each other.

MULVANEY

Yes, Sir. I understand, you understand. But
I'm not sure he understands ... or is
inclined to. He's got a different agenda, a
different point of —

TRUMP

I want us to meet out there somewhere.

MULVANEY

In Korea? I don't think that would be wise,
Mister President. Tough logistics. If we
were on better terms with China, if we
resolved our trade issues with them, they

ACT THREE

might be willing to broker a meeting at a neutral site.

TRUMP
No. China is a big, big trading problem for us. I'm going to keep the pressure on them. Heavy, heavy pressure. They'll give in. They need our business. Xi knows they need us more than we need them. They'll settle. That's how you make deals, Mick, by making it painful for the other side until they cave. Showing them who has the stronger hand, the bigger stick.

MULVANEY
(Nodding slowly) Meeting face to face with Kim, especially if it meant going over there, might be more to his benefit than to ours, to yours, Mister President.

TRUMP
Well, I can't very well invite him to the White House, can I? Set up a channel so I can communicate with him. I'll negotiate with him, make a deal with him. After all, he let that young man, that Warmbier fellow, come home.

MULVANEY
Barely alive, Sir. A breathing corpse, essentially. This time a two million dollar corpse. Trying to deal with Kim is not —

TRUMP
I'm not going to try, Mick. I'm going to do it. And I'm going to sit down with Putin as well, have long private talks with both of them.

ACT THREE

MULVANEY

Yes, Sir.

TRUMP

There are things I have to do, Mick. I need your help, not your okay.

MULVANEY

Yes, Sir. Of course, Mister President.

TRUMP

I understand them. I can handle both of them. They each have things they want and I can make a deal with each of them.

> (TRUMP faces audience, moves slowly downstage.)

TRUMP
"I'LL HANDLE THEM"

I'm the smart one, the most smart one,
So both will be putty to me.
Despite what some in Congress may say
I'll set them straight, as you'll see.
Why just the other day on Fox
They said I was the one
Who this country sorely needed.
There's no doubt I'll get it done.

Putin's my friend,
And Kim is my friend.
They're both used to using fear.
I'll handle them; I'll handle them.
I'll make deals with them
And not give a thing away.

ACT THREE

I'll handle them; I'll handle them.
I'm better at deals than them.
So I won't give a thing away.
The trick's to handle them,
To deal with them and to manage them
And not give a thing away.

TRUMP
You start setting up those meetings. I'll
write Kim a letter, a beautiful, perfect
letter and let him know we can make a deal.

STAGE GOES DARK. LIGHTS UP ON KOREAN FEMALE
VOCAL FOLK MUSIC QUARTET, IN STRIKING RED
ETHNIC DRESS.

MUSIC: (MINYO "SAETARYEONG - SONG OF BIRDS")

TRUMP, JACKET OPEN AND LONG TIE FLOWING, AND
KIM JONG-UN, IN BLAND OUTFIT, APPEAR ON
OPPOSITE SIDES OF STAGE.

> (TRUMP and KIM slowly walk toward
> each other, KIM's **INTERPRETER**
> follows.)

MUSIC CONTINUES, SOFTLY.

> (KIM, smiling broadly, points down
> and makes a sweeping gesture to point
> out the boundary line. TRUMP steps
> across. KIM accompanies TRUMP into
> North Korean territory, where they
> shake hands warmly.)

FOLK SONG MUSIC FADES.

ACT THREE

TRUMP

It's wonderful, very wonderful that we're
meeting again and that we're meeting here,
right here where our conflicts need to be
resolved and our talks need to resume.

KIM

(Speaks Korean)

INTERPRETER

(Turning from KIM to TRUMP) I never expected
to meet you in this place.

TRUMP

I wanted this to happen. I'm proud to step
over the line.

> (Side by side, they pat each others'
> backs as they walk toward Freedom
> House.)

TRUMP

Now, let's talk. Let's have a good, serious
talk before our teams get down to work.

FOLK MUSIC (INSTRUMENTAL ONLY) BUILDS AND
STOPS ABRUPTLY. STAGE DARK.

LIGHTS UP ON EMPTY OVAL OFFICE.

> (TRUMP enters, holding up several
> sheets of paper, the rotund secretary
> of state, **MIKE POMPEO** follows, with
> MICK MULVANEY close behind. All
> remain standing.)

TRUMP

(Waving the papers) Kim has written me a
beautiful, beautiful letter. That short-
sighted Kelly said he wasn't to be trusted.
He got that wrong, never understood much

about managing people. It was him[sic] that[sic] wasn't to be trusted. He didn't appreciate what I could get done. I wonder how many more overrated Generals I've been stuck with? (Reflects, then waves letter more vigorously.) See Mike? I've showed we could get it done, get peace moving over there.

(POMPEO nods silently)

MULVANEY
Quite a good step forward, Sir.

TRUMP
Well, it was just a matter of knowing how to negotiate, something that *General* Kelly was not equipped for. He was another one I should never have hired. (Waves letter) Finally, peace for the peninsula, in my time.

POMPEO
I'd like to suggest, Mister President, that we be cautious in dealing with Kim. He's not a pushover. He's had years of training and has a dedicated, dependent cadre of supporters over there.

TRUMP
So?

POMPEO
He's proud, he's confident, and he's more than a little vicious. I would say nothing is off the table for him. It's been surprising how far they've come with their weapons programs in such a short time.

ACT THREE

TRUMP

Well, it looks like we'll get an agreement, a good and favorable agreement. That speaks for itself.

TRUMP
"MY BUDDY SENT ME THIS LETTER"

I've shown them all I could get it done.
I negotiated far better than anyone.
Kim's rockets will be still.
He's bending to my will.
My buddy sent me this letter.

You should read what little Kim has to say.
He's come around to see things just my way.
Peace is now the plan
After talking man to man.
My buddy sent a beautiful letter.

Now Kim sent me this letter,
Wrote he wants to be part of the world once more.
He agrees that there's much good to foresee.
And he should not threaten our shore.
Beautiful, so beautiful.

ACT THREE

This's an open, positive message to me.
Those war games were bad, I certainly
do agree.
I had to pay;
I hated that anyway.
My buddy penned a very fine letter.

I'll get those weapons talks to start again.
There'll be no need to pound like angry
men.
He sees things my way.
North and South will be okay.
My buddy put this all in his letter.

> (MULVANEY, puts cell phone to his
> ear, grimaces.)

So Kim sent me this letter,
Wrote he wants to be part of the world
once more.
He took time to write that there's no
need to fight,
And he won't threaten our shore.
Beautiful, so beautiful.

History will tell how it got done,
How I negotiated better than anyone.
Kim's rockets will be still.
He's bending to my will.
My buddy wrote me a fine letter.
Kim's rockets will be still.
He's bending to my will.

ACT THREE

My buddy has sent me this letter.
Yes, my buddy wrote a beautiful letter.

TRUMP
What wrong, Mick?

MULVANEY
North Korea's just launched some missiles.
To the east, toward Japan. They are short
range test flights, we judge. Reporters are
on the lawn.

TRUMP
So? They're short range. Not ballistic
tests; not long-range missiles. Nothing's
changed. Everything's fine, fine. He's sent
me a beautiful, beautiful letter. You know
why he did that? It's because he's smart and
he knows I'm *very* smart. Smart people always
work well together.

POMPEO
Yes. Kim's smart. Mister President.

MULVANEY
(To TRUMP) Not as smart as you, Sir, of
course.

POMPEO
Correct. Clever might be the better word. He
sends signals as well as words. We have to
be very careful in deciding which are
significant.

TRUMP
We can get along. Two smart people getting
along beautifully. Read my tweets. Even
though the Fake Media is focused on
their[sic] agenda rather than the truth,
they admit that I'm very, very smart. A

-107-

ACT THREE

genius. Smart people want to be around me and work with me. It's better working with smart people. Stupid people are unpredictable.

POMPEO
Sir. Yes, Sir.

TRUMP
You can't rely on them.

MULVANEY
No, Sir.

TRUMP
Now, if we can get past these impeachment hearings, that collusion delusion hoax, maybe this will shut Pelosi and her media cronies up, for good. It'll be my revenge. The country is on my side. You can tell that they love me, no matter what.

STAGE DARK.

LIGHTS UP ON HOUSE HALLWAY. REPRESENTATIVE **JIM JORDAN** TALKING TO A GROUP OF REPORTERS. HE IS ENERGETIC, JACKETLESS, AND ANGRY.

REPORTER
Mister Jordan, have you any comment on the way these hearings have progressed?

JORDAN
Progressed? That's funny. RE-gressed is more like it.

REPORTER
Follow up - Would you say a credible case for impeachment has been made?

ACT THREE

JORDAN

Credible? No. In fact, it's laughable. What have we gotten from this circus? Nothing. Nothing except for a public display of the same false narrative that the Democrats have been pushing for months. Hours and hours of talk; pages and pages of testimony; a stacked crowd of witnesses all marching to nothing, for nothing. There's no proof of a crime. Not even credible suspicion. Just their own partisan and false narrative. Yes, you've asked the right question: After their parade of witnesses and the waste of bushels of tax payer money, what have we got?

JORDAN
"WHAT DID THEY FIND?"

Some people will claim that he's done much that is bad.
I'm here to say he's the best that we've had,
The best that we've had, to move the country along.
I'm pleased to be the one to root him on with this song.

They took nearly two years and what did they find?
Absolutely nothing of substance, no guilt of any kind.
Big money's been spent, many witnesses on parade,
But at the end of the day, all there's been is charade.

ACT THREE

I bought cattle to raise on our farm in the West,
Learned you got how you gave, and to hell with the rest.
I've been eager to boost what those in my district demand.
Republican farmers, you see, know what's best for the land.

    (JORDAN pulls out several pompoms and waves them as he continues.)

The hearings drone on and what have we got?
Absolutely nothing of substance, just the Democrats' rot.
Time and money's been spent, witnesses put on parade,
But at the end of the day, all there is is charade.

Witnesses lie. They do it all the time.
Those with agendas think that that is no crime.
"Never Trump" is clearly what some of them choose.
And that's on them, what you should report in the news.

ACT THREE

The hearings're on TV but what have
they shown?
Nothing of substance, just dogs at a
bone.
Right, a fortune's been spent,
witnesses put on parade,
But at the end of the day, all there
is, is charade.

After all this effort tell me what did
they find?
Absolutely nothing of substance, no
guilt of any kind.
Read the transcripts yourselves, then
you'll easily see,
The only judgment is that this farce
ought not to be.

> (JORDAN pauses to reflect, then
> resumes waving the pompoms more
> energetically.)

Some people will claim that he's done
much that is bad.
I'm here to say he's the best that
we've had.
The best that we've had, to move the
country along,
So I'm pleased to be the one to root
him on with this song.

ACT THREE

(JORDAN turns. Waving the pompoms, he
struts away with the reporters close
behind.)

Some people will claim that he's done
much that is bad.
I'm here to say he's the best that
we've had,
The best that we've had, to move the
country ahead.
Help me put out the truth and stand
this hoax on its head.

(Fade and repeat as they moves off
stage.)

Help me put out the truth and stand
this hoax on its head.

OVAL OFFICE. A VISIBLY ANGRY TRUMP ENTERS,
FOLLOWED BY MIKE POMPEO. TRUMP SITS HEAVILY.
POMPEO REMAINS STANDING IN FRONT OF DESK.

TRUMP
They're going to impeach me! Can you
imagine??? It's a crime, a terrible,
terrible crime. These impeachment hearings
are a disaster for the country. Yes, perhaps
even treason. How can they be doing this?
After all I've done? It's the best three
years that our country has ever had, that
any President has ever had! Look at the
record. Pelosi and her rotten crowd are
trying to subvert an election. That's not
the way a democracy is supposed to be run.
It's terrible for democracy. They should
change the name of their party. Democracy is

the very opposite of what they're doing.
They have no right to use that word to name
their party. It's treasonous, obviously
treasonous, don't you think?

POMPEO
(After a brief pause to make sure TRUMP is
done) Pretty close to that, I believe,
Mister President. Yes. But I think you
should put it in perspective. After all,
they've been working up to this ever since
you took office. The Ukraine? Really?

TRUMP
That's what they're screaming about. My call
to its President. That perfect, perfect
call.

POMPEO
It's Democratic bull ... It's a joke, Sir.
The American people don't know of or care
about the Ukraine ... Couldn't name one of
its major cities ... They couldn't even find
it on a map!

TRUMP
True. Very, very true. Only that Pelosi nag
seems to care about the Ukraine. And not
even care! She's found something to make a
nonsensical fuss over and is just using it.

POMPEO
They didn't give you even that first one
hundred before attacking you. Keep in mind,
Sir, it's what they do. They're the
opposition and are just being more
underhanded than usual. They've been quite
happy to spread lies and make a lot of
noise. That's all it is, Mister President.

ACT THREE

TRUMP

(Gesturing angrily) They should be called the UN-democratic party!

POMPEO

Sir, I'd advise that you not take this personally. It's D.C. politics, how the Hill works. Don't let it distract you. As you said, Mister President, she's simply using it as cover for their partisan attacks. They've found an empty barrel and are pounding on it to make as much noise as they can.

POMPEO
"IT'S NOISE"

You can tell it's noise,
From Pelosi's fake news toys.
Who've gone rogue, rogue, rogue.
Simply rogue, rogue, rogue.

She thinks they'll turn back the clock,
But there is no way.
Your plan's here to stay.
Here to stay.

This impeachment trash is almost funny.
Means nothing to our folks.
They know it's a hoax.
Just lies, lies, lies.
Lies, lies, lies.

ACT THREE

So think of it as noise,
From Pelosi's fake news toys.
Who've gone rogue, rogue, rogue,
And tell lies, lies, lies.

You've so many on your side.
Her words won't play.
You're here to stay.
Here to stay.

Fox and Friends has so much to say,
The Senate dare not flag.
So it's in the bag.
In the bag.
Yes. Oh, yes. In the bag.
You're here to stay.

So all the rest is noise,
From Pelosi's fake news toys.
Who've gone rogue, rogue, rogue.
Tell lies, lies, lies.

Yes, all this fuss is noise,
From Pelosi's fake news toys.
Who like to lie, lie, lie.
Simply lie, lie, lie.

Graham's content to head up the charge
While Jordan cheers them on.
So the problem will be gone.
Gone, gone, gone.

ACT THREE

Sure the Dems will storm and shout.
That won't matter anyway.
It'll end up your way.
End up your way.
Yes, your way. Your way.
You're here to stay.

So, please ignore the noise
From Pelosi's fake news toys.
It's all lies, lies, lies.
Partisan lies, lies, lies.

Best ignore the noise,
From Pelosi's party cronies.
It's all lies, lies, lies.
Partisan lies, lies.
It's all lies, lies, lies.
Partisan lies, lies, lies.

TRUMP AND POMPEO GO STATIC. OVAL OFFICE
DIMS. LIGHTS UP OUTSIDE ROOM 1100, THE HOUSE
INTELLIGENCE COMMITTEE'S MEETING ROOM. ADAM
SCHIFF IS SPEAKING TO A TIGHT GROUP OF
REPORTERS. LINDSEY GRAHAM IS IN BACKGROUND.

SCHIFF
(Earnest and serious) The last thing we
would wish to be spending our time on is an
impeachment hearing. Absolutely, these
proceedings are an unfortunate use of
valuable time. However, he's a President
unbound. You could not have a more open-and-
shut case of obstruction of Congress. As
Speaker Pelosi has said, it has to be done.
It is as if he wants this to happen, that he

ACT THREE

wants to be impeached so that he can use it to marshal his supporters. The President doesn't give a shit about what's good for this country, what's good for Ukraine. It's all about what's in it for him, personally and for his reelection campaign. That's a perfect summary of where we are. He blames and complains; he insults and creates tumult; he provides no evidence that the misdemeanors he's accused of did not take place or are insufficient. He simply now revises reality as it suits him. However, both he and his advisors had admitted, on numerous occasions, to the facts we've presented. The President's strategy with everything is basically the same: Don't defend misconduct; attack anyone who stands up to him. His and his advisors' attacks on truth have always seemed to me the most corrosive to our democracy, the idea that there's no such thing as fact anymore.

> (He nods several times, as if thinking what to say next.)

He's a difficult man.

SCHIFF
"PLAGUEY, PROLIX PRESIDENT"
(REPRISE OF "PRESCIENT, POTENT PRESIDENT")
Trump's a pompous presentiment of a plaguey, *prolix President.*
With much to say but little sense, it's sad he runs our government.

> (SCHIFF pauses, looks at his notes, then puts them aside.)

ACT THREE

Like those with misophonia, he finds
pain where most find pleasure.
He turns what's real into a lie; he
abases truth at leisure.
His economic views are quite strange,
some frankly seem hilarious.
When those schooled give wise advice,
they find he's quite impervious.
No Janus, he, a warming Earth's nothing
more than left wing terror.
He claims that coal is here to stay; in
glaciers' melt finds gross error.

In business, yes, Trump made a mark and
all the while he's had much fun.
But as our Chief Executive, he behaves
much like a coarse Sinon.
His storms of tweets that wreak of bile
should not be part of government.
He is a pompous presentiment of a
plaguey, prolix President.

(GRAHAM, lips tight, folds his arms
across his chest.)

East Germany had built its wall, part
of Russia's Iron Curtain.
To keep us out was partly true; to keep
them in was certain.

ACT THREE

Those enemies are now Trump's friends;
he acts though there's not history.
If I thought he'd accept her words, I'd
call upon Mnemosyne.
Professing love for pretty things,
especially fems with longish limbs,
He's bedded some and wedded some, paid
much so they'd give in to him.
Some are quick to claim they see
compensatory misogyny.
Clearly bored by staid monogamy, he yet
rejects misogamy.

Dunning-Kruger describes him well. His
main aim is his reelection.
Quick to pout, he's a rodomont who
rages at defection.
Creating tweets that make no sense
deeply impugns our government.
He is a pompous presentiment of a
plaguey, prolix President.

(GRAHAM scowls)

Trump's fond of touting all he's built,
his name in bold on every one.
In part this comes from besting Fred,
being more than a wealthy father's son.
To be impeached will be a blow, but his
career is full of those.
He's practiced at the gambler's art of
masking failure with a pose.

ACT THREE

He's called Zelensky for his aid to
tarnish an opponent's name.
Putin, too, was in that mix; he even
told Xi to "Do the same."
No matter what will some day come,
Trump is bent on fighting back.
Uplifted by Fox moirologists, he has no
need for truth or fact.

As presidents go he's not unique, but
certainly he's changed the mold.
Our history going forward will no doubt
differ from our old.
Still, by standing up to Trump we hope
to heal our government.
For he is a pompous presentiment of a
plaguey, prolix President.

Trump sees in each who disagrees
another hurtful enemy.
Witnessing coarse chirocracy makes us
fear for our democracy.
We can't help but think that such a man
as head of state is dangerous.
To claim it's simply politics is
clearly disingenuous.
The Constitution as our guide, we'll
use logic to make our case.
His telic tweets are far from that, are
clearly meant to rouse his base.

ACT THREE

*He may choose to condemn and blame but
the facts will yet come out.
Even he can't stop truth no matter how
long and loud he shouts.*

> (GRAHAM angrily paces, gesturing as
> if to cast his wrath upon SCHIFF.)

*To sum up what we all have seen, he's
broken his once solemn oath.
We cannot let this moment pass and lose
the chance of hearing truth.
We're done with tweets that rant and
rave; that's not a form of government.
Trump is a pompous presentiment of a
plaguey, prolix President.*

*We're done with tweets that rant and
rave; that's not a form of government.
Trump is a pompous presentiment of a
plaguey, prolix President.*

[OPTIONAL INSERTION: GRAHAM AND SCHIFF
REPEAT PORTIONS OF THEIR RESPECTIVE VERSIONS
IN UNISON, CREATING TOTAL CACOPHONY.]

STAGE DARK. LIGHTS UP ON STEPHEN MILLER AND
TRUMP WALKING TOWARD A TIGHT GROUP OF MAGA
SUPPORTERS SITTING ON STADIUM SEATS, WHICH
ARE SLOWLY DOLLIED FORWARD.

TRUMP
Is it a big crowd? Another beautiful, big
crowd?

ACT THREE

MILLER

Yes, Sir. The arena is packed. I made sure
that plenty of people were stacked up
outside as well. Just to be sure.

TRUMP

Good. Good. And they've the hats and signs
and all that?

MILLER

Certainly, Sir. Hats, jackets, placards,
everything as usual. They were warmed up
with videos and music. They'll be very
receptive.

TRUMP

Good. I need all the popular support I can
get. That crazy Pelosi woman is intent on
canceling 2016, making it as if I didn't win
big, as if my election never took place. Can
you imagine? I can't let her get away with
that. What she's doing is like a coup. It's
criminal. She and her media gang are
criminals and should be thrown in jail for
all their lies!

MILLER

That's not going to happen, Sir. They can't
undo a vote of the people, your people. They
can't take away their right to vote.

TRUMP

It's really all Sessions' fault. He started
this charade by running off instead of
supporting me. You worked for him. Weren't
you surprised when he did that?

MILLER

I was. Certainly, Mister President. He
should not have recused himself. He owed you
more loyalty than that.

ACT THREE

TRUMP

And then they dig up that Mueller guy. Get
him to run a phoney investigation! Sessions
ran off and then Rosenstein plucked Mueller
from ... from ... I don't know where. What a
hoax he's put over. Imagine. The Democrats
want to overturn an election, that's all
this is. That's absolutely all this is.
Instead of governing and making the country
great, they want to turn back the clock.

MILLER

Yes, Sir. You're absolutely right. We need
to have our people take that up and run with
it. The Democrats are running backwards,
trying to destroy this country.

TRUMP

The people don't want this impeachment
circus! I can see that in the polls. I want
it probably more than they do. It'll give me
a big boost in November, so I don't mind.
But what the Democrats are doing is a
tragedy for the country. A terrible,
terrible tragedy. Look at the kind of people
they let speak for them: Omar, Ocasio-
Cortez, Tlaib. These people shouldn't be in
the House. They shouldn't even be *here*.
They've got shit-hole countries that need
them far, far more than we do. They should
go back where they came from. We'd *all* be
better off.

MILLER

These rallies will get that across, Mister
President. We have plenty of time to make
sure we make that loud and clear. Plenty of
time for rallies. This is a good day for
one.

ACT THREE

MILLER
"GOOD TIME FOR A WHITE RALLY"

Who, Mister President, moans over what
you've done?
Who, Mister President, wants to turn
our country brown?
Who, Mister President, blocks at every
turn?
Who, Mister President, seeks what they
can't earn?

Sir, Mister President, chosen one,
It's a good time to have our say.
It's a good time for a white rally.
It's a good time to tell again ...

True, Mister President, fake news's
packed with lies.
True, Mister President, a White House
spoilt by spies.
True, Mister President, the Dems dream
to take you down.
But, Mister President, you're master of
this town.

You, Mister President, are the chosen
one.
It's a good time to seize the day.
It's a good time for a white rally.
It's a good time to start again.

ACT THREE

Now, Mister President, we'll turn Dems'
win into a loss.
Now, Mister President, make them see
who's boss.
Now, Mister President, bring the Hill
back to Right.
Now, Mister President, ensure our
country stays quite light.

Yes, Mister President, chosen one.
It's a good time to make them pay.
It's a good time for a white rally.
It's a good time to say again.

It's a good time to seize the day.
It's a good time for a white rally.
It's a good time to start again.

It's a good time to have our say.
It's a good time for a white rally.
It's a good time to tell again ...

TRUMP
Don't say it, Stephen. No need. No need. The
Russia thing and all that came from it is a
hoax, a huge, huge waste of time and
taxpayers' money. That's all we need tell
them. Mueller's report completely exonerated
me. No collusion. Absolutely no collusion.
They're putting on this impeachment show on
account of me simply having a perfect,
perfect long talk with Zelensky. It's what
world leaders do: Talk with each other. That
Schiff is a very sick man, a deranged human

being to make something bad out of a simple
phone call between two Presidents. It was a
perfect, perfect call. No quid pro quo. A
nothing. A perfect call. But I'll turn it
back at them — Pelosi and her treasonous
gang. Next month, when we get to the Senate,
it'll finally be the end of this collusion
delusion created by the Never Trumpers. Yes.
I'll turn it back onto the Democrats, get my
revenge, and make them pay at the polls!

TRUMP
"THE BEST DEFENSE IS ALWAYS TO ATTACK"
MUSIC: MOZART'S *MAGIC FLUTE* - PAPAGENO'S
"VOGELFÄNGER" SONG

(Sprightly) To lead this land I'm
clearly the best.
No other President can pass my test.
I am the master of the art of the deal.
I am the decider of what's real.
(He is the decider of what's real.)

So for each crime they do accuse me of,
You can sense the rise of even firmer
love.
No matter what they say, I shout it
back.
The best defense is always to attack.

I make good use of my Teflon suit.
However I'm accused it ends up moot.

ACT THREE

I'll indict the indictors, who are out
on a limb.
Complaints slide from me but stick to
them.
(Complaints slide from him but stick to
them.)

Pelosi and her gang are out to see me
gone.
It's not working for them, my support's
too strong.
For no matter what is said, I'll shout
it back.
The best defense is always to attack.

Experience has taught me and Rudy
agrees,
What one believes is more than what one
sees.
The stranger the story the more it must
be told.
Fox Friends and tweets are getting it
sold.
(Fox Friends and tweets are getting it
sold.)

When November comes along I'll be on a
roll.
That next time you'll see it obvious in
the polls.

*Yes, no matter what is said, I shout it
back.*
The best defense is always to attack.

*For no matter what'll be said, I'll
shout it back.*
The best defense is always to attack.

TRUMP
Now, I need to get over there and hear how
much they love me. Let them show it again.

MILLER
Of course, Mister President. I'll lead the
way.

(MAGA crowd chanting and roaring in
background)

TRUMP
Hear that?. Those are my people. They love
me.

RAILED PLATFORM AT REAR OF STAGE, LIT WITH
BROAD SPOTS FROM EITHER SIDE. WALL BEHIND
DECORATED WITH AMERICAN FLAGS AND BUNTING.
MAGA SUPPORTERS ARRAYED IN FRONT, THEIR
BACKS NOW TO AUDIENCE.

(TRUMP appears on platform. MAGA
SUPPORTERS wave hats and placards,
chant their affection.)

**MUSICAL BACKGROUND: START OF ACT THREE, *DIE
WALKÜRE*, BY WAGNER. VERY SOFT.**

(TRUMP paces across the platform. He
stops, stands proudly, looking out

(and scanning his SUPPORTERS,
acknowledging their response.)

(In short bursts TRUMP confidently
and comfortably orates to his crowd.
Becoming interspersed with the
Wagnerian musical background, each
spoken word or phrase is isolated and
meant to represent part of a longer,
mimed statement, to which his
SUPPORTERS give noisy expressions of
disdain and/or support.)

TRUMP

... impeachment ... (Booo ...)

... undo an election ... (Boooo ...)

... I'm your guy ... (Hooray ...)

... great again! (Yayyy ...)

... corrupt media say ...(No, no ...)

... and Fake News ... (Lies! Booooo ...)

... socialist liberals ... (Booo ...)

... traitors! (Booooooo!!!)

CRESCENDO AT POINT WHERE VALKYRIES VOCALIZE,
THEN MUSIC FADES.

(TRUMP grasps rail and scans the
crowd.)

TRUMP
The House Democrats have voted to impeach
me. Crazy, crazy. It's a stain upon
democracy. But I was willing to be
impeached. You and America deserve that I

stand up to that pack of D.C. wolves. I was
willing to be impeached. I've been wanting
it. I've been waiting for it. Pelosi and the
others of her crowd have made a very, very
bad mistake. They are not smart people at
all. Not very smart. No, not very smart
politicians. Come November we're going to
show them how big their mistake was!

(Loud roar from crowd)

The Demo-rats made a big mistake!

(Another loud roar)

A big, big mistake. It all started with that
Mueller hoax. All the Democrats in the House
accomplished was to waste so, so much time
and money - Congress's time and *your* money.
Terribly, terribly large amounts of time and
money were wasted. For what? Nothing!

(SUPPORTERS roar approval, wave hats
and banners.)

TRUMP
The Inspector General, Horowitz, whitewashed
what the FBI did and still came up with
nothing. Nothing. There is no crime. No
crime. I am the first person to ever get
impeached and there is no crime! I feel
guilty. You know what they call it?
"Impeachment lite." I don't know about you,
but I'm having a good time!

(SUPPORTERS roar, standing to wave
their hats, placards, and banners.)

TRUMP

But that Horowitz. Sometimes I don't
understand those people. I've worked with
them on many, many deals and I still don't
understand them. He's acting like a
Democrat. Really. Can you believe that? A
Democrat, like those that[sic] control the
House. (Booo.) I think any Jewish people
that[sic] vote for a Democrat, I think it
shows either a total lack of knowledge or
great disloyalty. Disloyalty is a terrible,
terrible thing.... It started right when I
was elected, with Sessions walking away and
his second at the Justice Department doing
what Sessions should have refused to do.
Sessions did more than go along with it. He
helped it! (Booo.) He helped it! (Nooo.
Booo!) He let his stand-in dig up that
Mueller guy to start a witch hunt! Barr's
the kind of man we need. We need more men in
government like Bill Barr!!

(Another, louder roar from the crowd)

BANNERS, OF REPUBLICAN RED, BEGIN TO UNFURL
ON THE WALL BEHIND HIM, OVERLAYING WHAT IS
ALREADY THERE.

DIE WALKÜRE RESUMES, SOFTLY BLENDING INTO
THE LAST FOUR MINUTES OF WAGNER'S
GÖTTERDÄMMERUNG, STARTING AT THE POINT AT
WHICH "THE VALKYRIES RIDE" LEITMOTIF
REAPPEARS.

TRUMP

There's a wolf pack in Congress that wants
to see me gone. "Never Trump!" They've been
screaming that for three years, for more
than three years really. Even before I was
elected ... by YOU! (Responsive roar)
America is being destroyed by them. They

ACT THREE

hate America and want to see it destroyed. And who are these people who hate America? Just listen to their names, the ones working with Pelosi: Omar, Ocasio-Cortez, Tlaib — Rashida Tlaib, can you imagine? — and Castro! Can you imagine that? Those are who are supposedly representing us??? And Democrats voted for them!

> (Crowd vigorously approves of his sarcasm.)

ORCHESTRAL MUSIC (*GÖTTERDÄMMERUNG*), STILL SUBDUED BUT BUILDING, STARTING FROM "ZURÜCK VOM RING"

TRUMP
And who's been putting out this Russian meddling hoax? This shameful, shameful witch hunt? And now, this impeachment? Who are the traitors working with Pelosi? I'll tell you: (In a slow, steady cadence) Cohen, Nadler, Raskin, Schiff, Yovanovich, Matz, (with derision) Feldman, Goldman! And where did this all start? Who was it that decided to let some retired bureaucrat — someone from the FBI, which was infested with Never Trumpers and Horowitz whitewashed — start a phoney investigation after Sessions turned his back on me? (With extreme derision) Rosenstein!!!

> (Supporters break into hoots then raucous laughter, followed by loud applause, cheers, and MAGA chants.)

TRUMP
Yes, you know who they are.... But I'll clean up the Washington swamp once and for all after next November. I'll have an unstoppable majority in Congress. I promise

ACT THREE

you that. Unstoppable. Come November, we'll
clean house and be rid of them, finally.
With your help we'll turn them all out and
start again. It'll be a Merry Christmas for
us, but not for them!!!

SUPPORTERS

Jail 'em, jail 'em ... Lock 'em up ... Send
'em home ... America is for Americans ...
America first ... America first ... America
for Americans!... God bless you, Donald ...
You're the One!

CYMBALS CRASH. THE RED BANNERS ARE NOW FULLY
UNFURLED AND COVER THE WALL BEHIND. EACH HAS
A POINTED BOTTOM, LIKE A NECKTIE, AND ARE
EMBELLISHED BY A BOLD CAPITAL "T" CENTERED
IN A PALE GRAY CIRCLE. LIGHT ON TRUMP FADES.
ONE BANNER AND ITS CENTERED, BLACK BLOCK "T"
IS HIGHLIGHTED.

STAGE SUDDENLY DARK, WITH LAST FEW BARS OF
GÖTTERDÄMMERUNG AT FULL VOLUME.

SUDDEN SILENCE.

END OF ACT THREE

EPILOGUE

LIGHTS UP. BEARDED MAN ON EMPTY STAGE.

BEARDED MAN
Wait. Don't leave.... Let me have final word
or two. You've plans and much yet to do, I
know, but hear me out.

> (BEARDED MAN puts on a battered red,
> white, and blue Uncle Sam hat.)

BEARDED MAN
I'm tickled by this hat. It was Allen
Ginsberg's incongruity but is so suited to
these times. (He fingers his chin.) People
use all kinds of strategies and props, you
know, to create their desired public
identity. Often the efforts do come off to
some as bizarre, even counterproductive.
Yet, as with him (he taps the brim of the
hat), Ginsberg, when reality intrudes, it
can be more self-serving to be judged
unconventional or imprudent rather than
incompetent or sociopathic. We'll hear a lot
about that during the 2020 presidential
campaign. Too much, perhaps. Nevertheless,
words and deeds can outlast their initiators
by many, many years. This is a perilous time
to accept masquerade. Deceptions must be
recognized. They must be challenged before
they become dogma. So ...

> (BEARDED MAN pulls out the red rubber
> ball once again but does not put it
> on. He bounces it on his hand as he
> scans the audience.)

EPILOGUE

BEARDED MAN
"IT'S UP TO YOU, REAL AMERICA"

... it's up to you, real America.
The nation needs you more than ever
now.
Please come together, real America,
Use your voice to get us turned around,
Before we run aground.

If you'll review our history you'll see
how much we've overcome.
Even at our start, democracy wasn't
guaranteed.
Financial woes and vicious wars have
taken bitter toll on some,
But many more stood their ground,
forsaking personal need.

Where has it gone, reasoned compromise?
Our nation needs that more than ever
now.
What's that you say, real America?
You do want that more than ever now?
Then make it show.

It's up to you, real America.
The nation needs you more than ever
now.
Please come together, real America,
Use your wits to get us turned around,
Before we run aground.

EPILOGUE

Anger and fear are always near but
that's not the way to govern.
Sadly we decry it but can't deny it's
become the style.
Some say hooray, others shout dismay,
which means we've still time to learn
What kind of democracy we're going to
have,
one built on honesty or on guile.

See? It's up to you, real America.
Our country needs you more than ever
now.
Come together, real America,
Use your energy to get us turned
around,
Before we run aground.

Using news to entertain never shines a
light.
Filling time and emptying our minds is
how we'll lose our way.
Many wrongs have gone on too long and
need to be set right.
Talk about them, protest against them,
don't let the lies slide by.

Don't take the bait and shrug okay
while the country's run for some.
Each of us has a stake in this, and all
must play their part.

EPILOGUE

After all whether good or bad, notable
deeds involve more than one.
Intellect is needed, that's true, but
we should not depose the heart.

Hat off to you, (he does so) real
America.
Our country needs you more than ever
now.
Come together, real America.
Stake your claim, get us turned around,
Before we run aground.

We must make our voices heard and move
those who sit in power.
If more want what we have now, then
that's just what we'll get.
It's been said and can be said again,
"This is a fateful hour."
I hope that most will feel not ready
for autocracy yet.

It's up to you, real America.
Our country needs you more than ever
now.
Please come together, real America,
Use your votes to get us turned around,
Before we run aground.

FADE TO DARK.

END

www.ingramcontent.com/pod-product-compliance
Lightning Source LLC
Chambersburg PA
CBHW020659260626
47157CB00008B/3092